The CARPE DIEM Plan ; God Had To Make A Choice

The CARPE DIEM Plan ; God Had To Make A Choice

God Had To Make A Choice

Andy Smith

TKR Publishing
Nashville, TN

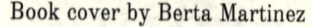

Book cover by Berta Martinez

Contents

Dedication

This book is dedicated to Mother Earth
With a sincere hope that someday
it will be non-fiction

Disclaimer

Boy that was a fun story to write. As a writer, there is nothing better than to simply trust your fingers on the keyboard without any clue of where you are headed. I knew my story would be about saving planet earth, but I also knew that I am not exactly the first person you would think of to come up with solutions for all the environmental issues we face. Not only am I not the sharpest pencil in the drawer, I'm more the pen that pretty much has no ink that you keep shuffling aside and have no idea why you keep it in the drawer in the first place.

But once you get the creative juices going, it becomes a great adventure for a writer to just jump into the water full of empty pages and come out with a story you hope that people can enjoy.

As I head to make myself a victory drink, I take note that my guardian angel, Chris, is not occupying my recliner in my living room. Thankfully, I will not have to debate with my guardian angel the merits of publishing this story as fiction.

But wait a minute.

We made a deal after I wrote *Hannah's Huggers* that he would only be here if God didn't want me to write a disclaimer. If Chris isn't here, that means God wants me to put a disclaimer at the beginning to suggest to my readers that God would prefer I publish the book as non-fiction.

Stupid angel probably forgot how it went.

I laugh it off because there is no way I need a disclaimer on this one. This story is totally fiction after all, right?

As I fix my drink and head back to my computer, I am startled to find Chris laying on my bed reading a magazine.

"Geeesh, Chris, you scared me. I'd prefer you be in my recliner when you come to visit me." I say as my pulse rate scrambles for a more mellow rhythm.

"Well I wasn't planning on being here until you accused me of being stupid and forgetting our deal." says the angel with a strong hint of displeasure.

"Well I understand. I had to think about it as well. If you're not here, it means I need the disclaimer that God would rather I publish it as a non-fiction. If you are here, it's to let me know that fiction is great with God and I do not need the disclaimer."

"Exactly. And that's why I wasn't in your recliner."

"See, you're still confused. There is nothing about this story that tells me it should be non-fiction."

"I would argue that you, sir, are the confused one. Although I will give you credit in thinking that this story could not be non-fiction, being that these events haven't actually occurred. But you need to know that God read your story and liked it very much and has decided that he may just use your story if things here on earth do not improve."

"So what kind of disclaimer is that going to be? You're telling me I need to tell all my readers that I published this book as fiction, but that God read it and really liked it, so he may steal the idea from me and use it if we don't get our act together? I can't write that."

"Well, buddy boy, I'm not here to argue with you or tell you what to say. We had a deal and I followed it exactly how we drew it up. I wasn't in the recliner because God would prefer you put in a disclaimer in the front of your book. How you word it is up to you. I'm just saying that like *7Days, Johnny's Story* and *Hannah's Huggers*, God looks at these stories as non-fiction and he looks at CARPE DIEM the same way. God doesn't want to throw any rocks, but if it comes to that, so be it. But God would rather see the earthlings take your story about saving planet earth very seriously."

With that, Chris is gone.

Note To Readers

This story is published by the author as fiction because it actually hasn't happened .…. YET… If you see any children talking to animals, you would be well advised pay attention to your environment and not laugh at the children. God knows how to throw rocks.

1

The Birth of CARPE DIEM

He had to make a decision.

We are at the Cloud Nine Assembly Hall in the Earth Operations section of Heaven. All guardian angels have been called together to hear God give his plan for planet Earth and there is a clear buzz of anticipation in the air.

God has been reviewing the situation on earth and there has been a lot of talk of what the creator will decide to do with the planet.

There are many angels who take the position that God needs to eliminate planet earth with a meteor as the earthlings have put the planet on course for a slow death with a lot of suffering, and have already reached the point of no return. They feel strongly that God should save the people from the increasingly dark period of suffering and show compassion by ending operations quickly.

But there are equally as many angels who caution that if God does end planet earth all at once, it would create too much chaos in Earth Operations trying to process every earthling at one time. They also argue that it was God who gave the earthlings a free will and it would be inconsistent for God to take matters into his own hands when he designed the planet to be a free will environment.

The pressure has been building for God to do something as the earth continues to spiral ever closer to a point of self-destruction. All the angels gathering are happy to know that God has finally made his decision and are anxious to begin implementing whatever plan he has come up with.

"Ladies and Gentlemen" says the announcer as the angels giggle and laugh as there are no ladies or gentlemen in the guardian angel program, but the announcer likes to be consistent with Earth Operations reflecting the lifestyle of the planet they represent.

"Please give a warm welcome to our own creator… the author of love … the God who put Earth on the map… your very own master of love-ins …. God Almighty!"

The angels break out in a joyous standing ovation as the band of Jimmi Hendrix and George Harrison on guitar, Dee Murray on bass, Hal Blaine on drums and Janis Joplin doing the vocals, start singing the Earth Operations theme of, "You Ain't Seen Nothin' Yet" as God slowly makes his way to the podium.

Personally, God does not get excited when he gives speeches at Earth Operations events as they always overkill the introductions. He'd rather just come out and start his speech, but the angels in Earth Operations like to reflect the planet they serve and nobody over produces an entrance better than the earthlings, so God just puts up with it.

As he patiently and politely waits for the music, dancing and joyous celebration to end, God admits to himself that the guardian angels really have put together a pretty awesome band and is not feeling that rushed to make them stop.

But stop they do, and as the angels gather back into their seats, God approaches the podium.

"Thank you all very much. Once again, Earth Operations has shown me that if there is one thing the earthlings can do, they sure know how to party."

The band breaks out in another verse of 'You Ain't Seen Nothin' Yet' as the angels start dancing and singing along, as God steps back realizing that the best thing he did was in not having any time value in heaven, as it appears that this assembly may take a while.

Again, the music and angels settle back down and God can sense that they are ready to move on.

"Thank you all for coming out today. As you are aware, Earth has been in trouble lately and it has reached a critical time for us to intervene. I have reviewed the situation with a strong desire to see what could be done to save planet Earth. I have reviewed all the options and have consulted with many of my assistants here at Earth Operations Headquarters.

I have approached this crises with a heavy heart because the bottom line is that I love planet Earth very much. It's not perfect, but I don't create any life on any of my planets to be perfect. I am fully aware that my policy of giving the creatures in charge of my planets a free will can create problems, as we see on Earth, but I am committed to a free will creation on every planet I create with life forms. I will never create a puppet world where I can merely pull strings and the creatures will do as I wish."

The angels applaud with enthusiasm.

"After a thorough review, I have come to the following conclusions:

"First, I must point out that I have never created a planet with life forms and later destroyed it. Yes, there have been instances where two planets have collided and been eliminated, but in these cases the issue has always been a miscalculation in the orbiting cycles and have been corrected by reassignment of assistants in charge of orbiting calculations.

"I have always maintained my relationship with all creatures in all my planets as a relationship built on unconditional love and will never compromise that love by throwing rocks at a planet and ending their existence because I don't like what they are doing.

"That will never happen!"

The angels again burst into an energized round of applaud.

"Secondly, after reviewing the situation on Earth, I have come to realize that the problems being created by the earthlings is not as wide spread as you would think. The true issue is that there are a small number of idiots who are in a position of power who are making decisions that are ruining the planets balance and putting all earthlings in a position of danger.

"In fact, I have been pleasantly surprised at the number of earthlings that continue to have good hearts and truly want to pursue a better life on the planet. I see a lot of good, strong hearts of love in spite of the problems they are facing. They simply don't have the power to make the changes.

"You guardian angels have done a very good job at keeping the spirits up on so many under the circumstances, and I commend you!"

The angels give themselves a standing ovation with many high-fives being passed around as the band cranks up another verse of 'You Ain't Seen Nothin' Yet'.

God stands back and lets the angel have their moment before he continues.

"So after my initial review, it was clear to me that I was not going to give up on planet Earth."

The angels burst into a euphoric atmosphere of celebration as the band plays a rock'n 'Try Just A Little Bit Harder' with Joplin killing the vocals.

God is in no hurry to settle this party down and seems to be enjoying the music that makes it nearly impossible for him to stand still. He does enjoy the party atmosphere that is a signature of Earth Operations events and he knows that he has made the right decision. Any planet that can party like that is not a planet you want to be throwing rocks at.

But it's time to move on, so God moves back to the podium to refocus the meeting.

"Thank you. I appreciate your enthusiasm and it is clear to me that only a fool would want to destroy a place that creates so much energy, music and passion. Unfortunately, there are fools who are destroying the planet and it is imperative that we come up with a plan now to get this planet back on track."

God pauses and looks at the angels with a big smile.

"And trust me, I have put together a plan that will put an end to the foolish decision makers and turn that planet onto a path of celebrating life like no other planet. A plan that will reward the many good hearts of earthlings who long for the days of living a balanced life. A plan that will bring a clear and strong message to anyone who dares to challenge…

"DO NOT MESS WITH MOTHER NATURE!!"

The angels go wild as the band bursts into a very energetic version of Harrisons 'Here Comes The Sun' as the assembly breaks into a party mode. George is blown away at Joplins vocals and how Jimmi's lead guitar has elevated his song from cute to rock'n party mode.

As the angels join in on every 'Here Comes The Sun' it is clear that once again God is thankful that there is no time issues on this side, and to be clear, even God is rather wrapped up in the Earth Operations musical offerings and doesn't seem in any hurry to move on.

But Janis needs a break to save her voice, so they close out this celebration as all the angels make their way back to their seats as God once again approaches the podium.

"Thank you. I do love the music here. If your band wants to hit the road, I have many planets that are lacking in emotions … They're good planets of course, but they have mostly smart creatures that don't quite have a handle on the emotional side of living. Their meetings for the most part are rather uneventful. I wouldn't mind taking this earthling band to open up for me at some of those meeting, that's all I'm say'n."

The angels and the band break into another celebration, this time letting Hendrix do his thing so Janis can rest her voice. But even the band senses that we need to move on, so they make an abrupt stop so God can continue.

God looks over to the band, "I'll take that as a yes." as the angels applaud with enthusiasm.

"But first things first. We need to get planet Earth back on track."

He pauses as he looks around the auditorium.

"Would the guardian angel for a miss Heather Baker please come up to the stage."

The angels all look around, when an angel in the middle of the auditorium stands and slowly makes it's way to the stage, with a clear case of apprehension.

"I promise you, this is going to be a good thing," God tells the angel as it draws nearer, then God looks out at the audience, "My angel looks as if I'm going to feed it to the lions." he smiles at the angel, "Relax, We're going to have some fun."

"Now, how long have you been Heather's guardian angel?"

The angel nervously says, "Since she was born."

God laughs – as does the many angels.

"Well I understand that. Tell us how old is miss Heather?"

"She has a birthday coming up and will be 9 years old." the angel states.

"You are correct," says God, "And I'm thinking you would agree with me that Heather is one special little girl, right?"

"Oh, yes God. She truly is a special girl. I hardly have to do anything to keep her on track."

"You are right again," says God as he turns to the angel, "Do you think she is that good because you are her angel, or do you think you are one lucky angel to land an assignment like Heather?"

The angel fumbles for an answer when God looks out to the audience.

"I'm sure it's a little of both." God says with a big smile as the angels applaud. "I know you angels love it when you get an assignment like Heather."

"I chose Heather after reviewing many hearts of the earthlings because she has a unique combination of compassion and intelligence that is exactly what we need for the plan I have developed. We are going to test out this plan with Heather because if she can't make the plan work, we may as well just give up and throw rocks at the planet."

The angels all gasp at the thought as God looks out over the gathering and smiles.

"Hey angels, keep in mind that I am God and I chose Heather because I have little doubt that when we gather again to evaluate how Heather did in her assignment, we are going to hear a whole lot more celebration from this band, and you can book it!"

The angels break into another enthusiastic applause before God holds up his arms to settle them back down.

"Okay, please sit down and let's talk about this plan." God waits for everyone to settle into their seats before continuing.

"I call this program the CARPE DIEM Program. As you all know, earthlings love to use acronyms so I thought I'd play along. Carpe Diem stands for 'Seize the Moment' which is exactly what we need to do now, but I also made it an acronym for my program:

"Children and Animals Rescue Planet Earth by Disarming the Idiots and Empowering the Many.

"I'm going to use the two best things I have created for planet Earth – Children and Animals. I will give the animal kingdom the ability of fully understand the voice of a child and be able to communicate with the children. Working together, the children and animals of the world will lead the way in taking back our Earth!"

The angels applaud as God turns to the angel standing next to him.

"Heather has a favorite stuffed animal, correct?" he asks.

"Yes. Marvin the Monkey. Marvin is with her always." says the angel.

God turns to the audience with a big smile.

"Ladies and Gentlemen, I'd like to introduce you to Marvin the Monkey."

He gestures to the angel who has a pained look of fear on his face as the angels applaud.

"Yes, as soon as this meeting is over, you will become Marvin the Monkey. You will un-stuff Marvin and re-stuff him with your very own self. You will talk to Heather, explain to her that you are her guardian angel and not a talking stuffed animal, fill her in on the assignment we have for her, and assure her that you will be with her throughout the assignment."

God smiles at Marvin, "Doesn't that sound cool?"

Marvin looks at God with uncertainty, "I don't know. What is the assignment?."

"Glad you asked, Marvin."

God pauses as he pulls up a picture of a zoo on the screen.

"This is the zoo in the city where Heather lives. It's a nice zoo – been there many times myself. They have good people working there and have been fighting the city to obtain some property next to the zoo for expansion. They want to develop a state-of-the-art reproduction center and medical research facility to work on endangered species. They can only do it if the city helps them out by donating the property or give a greatly discounted price to the zoo foundation."

He pulls up another picture, this time of a man sitting in his very fancy office which clearly indicates he is a very successful man who enjoys a great view of the city from atop one of the city's skyscrapers.

"This gentleman is named Nick Forsythe. He has made a handsome living building hotels and businesses in the city.

Not many people like him, as he seems to only concern himself with making money more than looking out for the best interests of the people. If Nick wants something, he's going to get it and he is the least concerned of who it might affect in doing so. Nick pretty much has the mayor and city council in his back pocket, as you don't win an election in this city without Nick's money backing you."

God pauses.

"This man is a good example of why planet Earth is so screwed up. His heart is controlled by greed."

"The issue is that Nick wants that property next to the zoo and has offered the city top dollar to re-zone the property so he can put in a large multiplex business with stores, restaurants and entertainment."

A collective sigh dances around the assembly hall.

"Well you don't have to be too smart to see where this is going. The city must decide between giving the property to the zoo to help the animals, or sell it to Nick for a nice profit and generate more revenue, jobs and votes for themselves."

"The zoo seems resolved to the reality that the city won't help them." God smiles broadly, "But they haven't met Heather, yet."

God pulls up another picture, this time of a cute girl.

"You see, it turns out that Nick has a daughter named Cathy. This is what she looks like. Cathy and Heather go to the same school and are pretty good friends."

"Now Marvin, your job will be to get Heather to get Cathy

to the zoo with her as soon as you can. The final vote for the property is in two weeks, so we don't have much time."

"I'm pretty sure that when young Cathy spends a day at the zoo talking to the animals and listening to Heather explain the reasons the animals are not very happy with her father, we might find the zoo in a better position to obtain that property, don't you think?"

The angels burst into applause with Marvin noticeably less enthusiastic than the others as he stands next to God with a frozen smile of fear.

"Now if this goes as I think it will," God pauses and smiles, "And as you all know I never lose a heart and I have no plans to start now."

Another outburst of applause.

"If this plan goes as it should, we will all gather here again and I will release all of you who are guardians of children to connect with your child and begin your assignment working with the animals. Those of you who are guardians of adults will be on high alert and monitoring your adults heart. At any time your adult's heart softens in support of the children and animals, you will immediately connect with your adult earthling, explain to them what is going on and recruit them to come up with a plan that will help the children and animals."

The excitement in the hall is explosive as God concludes.

"Marvin will stay with me for a more detailed plan with Heather, but the rest of you now know what the plan is." He pauses with another smile, "Throwing a rock and ending planet Earth was the easy answer... Teaming up with the children and animals was the fun answer... and I assure you all – this is one God that will always chose the fun answer.

"ARE YOU READY TO TAKE BACK PLANET EARTH?"

The band explodes into "You Ain't Seen Nothin' Yet" as the crowd of angels burst into dance and celebration as God walks Marvin the monkey off stage.

God had to make a decision.

Game on!

~~~~~~~~~~

As the celebration shows no signs of wrapping up out in the assembly hall, God and Marvin settle into the green room back stage to nail down the details.

"So I'm guessing you might have a few questions." God smiles at Marvin.

"Well sir, the plan sounds good – I do like the idea of using children and animals, for sure. So what exactly am I suppose to do with Heather?"

"Well Marvin (God loves it when an angel takes on a name for an assignment), after your initial visit of getting Heather use to the idea that her favorite stuffed animal is now possessed by her guardian angel and talks to her, you will explain to her that we need her to take Cathy to the zoo and help her talk to the animals and understand that the zoo animals are not very happy with her father and they need her to help change her fathers mind about the property."

Marvin looks hesitant as God continues.

"You see, Marvin, once we get Cathy on board with saving the planet, we can have her bug her father to take her to the zoo. Maybe one her favorite animals just had a baby and she wants to go see it or something. Whatever you can work out, we just need to get Nick and Cathy to the zoo."

God pauses to let this sink in.

"Now on the day that Nick and Cathy go to the zoo, all the animals will be on the same page and will know that when they see Nick approaching their exhibit, they are all going to turn around and do nothing. I want Nick to see nothing but fannies all day long."

God leans forward with a big smile, "I would totally be okay if the Rhinos took a dump while Nick is watching their fannies – no one pays more for the human stupidity than the Rhinos, that's for sure."

Marvin is humored and laughs, "Yes sir."

"Since Cathy will be in on the plan, she will understand what the animals are doing and can play a dramatic role in asking her father why the animals don't like her. I think you should also have some people around who can take pictures of the animals turning their backs on Nick Forsythe which should go viral on social media, I would think. Especially if there are pictures from many different sources of animals at all the exhibits turning their backs on Nick during his visit."

Marvin is now sitting up and taking this all in.

"We can also have the guardian angels of the adults who love what the animals are doing to Nick be contacted and recruited to help the children and animals in their fight to save the animals."

God sits back with a big smile.

"But isn't that kind of cheating? I mean, we are kind of interfering with a free will program." asks Marvin.

God smiles, "No, it's not cheating because I'm the creator. I can't cheat on my own creation, but I can change the rules at any time. I want that property to go to the animals, not that greedy, heartless businessman and since it's my creation, I plan on getting my way, Marvin."

"But what if they still sell it to Nick?" asks Marvin.

"Well, like you say, it is a free will planet and they certainly have made many bad choices in the past – that's why we have to do this in the first place. But I've studied Heather and Cathy's hearts. I have also looked closely at Nicks heart. I have every reason to think that this is going to be a great victory for the animals and be just the beginning of a movement all over the world by children and animals to get this planet headed on a better path of harmony."

Marvin sits back inspired and much more relaxed with the assignment.

"I can see how this can be a great start for the CARPE DIEM Program. I know I'm biased, but picking Heather to get this program started was a great choice. I think she's going to make you proud, God."

God smiles at Marvin, "Children always make me proud. It's the adults that wear my patience thin."

"Well God, unless you have anything else for me, I think I'm ready to go." says Marvin.

"Just remember that as you are with Heather every step of the way, I will be with you. If you have any concerns, know that you are my top priority right now."

"I promise. I'm not going to let this assignment fail."

God smiles at Marvin with compassion, "Be a good monkey."

With that, Marvin disappears and the CARPE DIEM Programs begins.

Decision made.

2

Marvin and Heather Create the Plan

'Are you kidding me,' says Marvin to himself, 'This kid is laying on top of me and has all her weight on me! I can't breath! She's crushing me, for crying out loud! God should have chosen a less popular stuffed animal, that's for sure.'

"Marvin, this is God. You do know that kids love to be tickled, right? Stop whining and get to work."

'I'm not whining, I'm dying down here!' says Marvin to himself, then pauses, 'Oh yeah, tickling might help.'

He looks around and sees that he is rather close to Heathers arm pit, so he maneuvers his arm and starts tickling her. Heather giggles and then grabs Marvin and holds him tight in her arm as she settles back into slumber land .

Now Marvin finds himself strangling from a tight headlock.

'Oh great! Now she's going to choke me to death. This assignment has disaster written all over it!'

"Marvin, this is God again. Please remember that you are

an angel and I have given you all powers necessary to get out of little jams like this."

'Little jams, he calls it? I'm dying and he calls it a little jam?! Oh yeah – I am an angel. I can't die."

Marvin gently, but powerfully, raises Heathers arm and wiggles his way to freedom and stands next to Heather on the bed with a proud sense of accomplishment.

As Heathers arm reaches for Marvin, the angel speaks for the first time.

" Oh no you don't." as he slaps her hands, Heather is startled awake.

"Now don't you dare scream, young lady, because your parents will come in here and you'll tell them that 'Marvin slapped my hand' and they will look at me all lifeless laying next to you and you will spend the rest of your life in and out of institutions known as the girl who thinks stuffed animals are real!"

"Marvin, God here … that's a bit thick, really."

Heather looks at Marvin with a curios face, "Who are you?"

"I'm Marvin the Monkey. But not the Marvin the Monkey you know, I'm actually your guardian angel inside Marvin the Monkey and I need to talk to you about an assignment that God wants you to help with."

Heather looks closely at Marvin and is thinking maybe she is still asleep and this is just a weird dream that she is having. Of course, being that Marvin is her guardian angel and knowing what your earthling is thinking is a pretty important tool in the guardian angel program, Marvin knows what Heather is thinking.

"This is not a dream, Heather. I really am your guardian angel and have taken over the body of Marvin the Monkey so I can talk to you and be with you throughout the assignment. But before we start, you must understand that only you can hear me or see any gestures I might make – everyone else will see me as Marvin the stuffed animal, okay?"

Heather is pinching her hand as if she's not totally convinced that this isn't a dream, then looks at Marvin, "So what do you want?"

Marvin relaxes as he sees that Heather is warming up to her talking stuffed monkey really being her guardian angel.

"I'm here to tell you about a plan God has to save the planet Earth, and he needs your help."

"Why does he want me? I'm just a kid."

"Oh trust me, girl. When God explained this program to me, I was totally blown away. I could see right away why he chose you for the assignment and there is no doubt in my mind that you and I are going to have an awesome time. Like that time when you were four and learning to ride a bike. Remember…"

"Marvin, God here. The plan please."

"Oh right – the plan."

Heather is amused at how her stuffed animal paces around the bed and shows so much enthusiasm. "So what does he want me to do?"

"Well Heather, you love animals, right?"

"Well if you're my guardian angel, you would already know that, right?" She says with a tone of sarcasm.

Marvin holds his arms up, trying to stay calm, "Stay with me, girl … stay with me … just answer the questions."

"And you love going to the zoo, right?"

"Yes" says Heather with a mocking sense of animated seriousness which Marvin could do without, but decides to keep moving.

"And you do know that the zoo has been working hard to raise enough money for the property next to them to build a big reproduction and medical research center, right?"

"Yes." she says emphatically.

"And you further understand that there is a Nick Forsythe who wants to buy that same property and turn it into a shopping multiplex venue, right?"

Heather's shoulders sag as her demeanor dampens, "He's not a nice man. His daughter tried to talk him into buying another property so the zoo could build there, but he didn't even listen to his own daughter." she says sadly.

"Exactly. And God wants you and Cathy to help in changing Mr. Forsythe's mind."

"Oh I don't think Mr. Forsythe is going to listen to us. He's ready to start building as soon as the council approves his plan."

Marvin smiles and looks right at Heather, "Well with God and all the animals at the zoo working with you and Cathy, I'm thinking he might listen to what you have to say."

Heather has a look of confusion, "All the animals at the zoo?"

Marvin smiles wider, "Yes, for this assignment, God is giving all the animals at the zoo the ability to hear and understand what you and Cathy say and they will be able to communicate with you, too."

"Cathy and I will be able to talk to the animals – and they will talk back?" Heather says when a bit of excitement.

"Yes, but remember this is all part of Gods plan, so we have to be discrete when we are talking to the animals because we don't want the people around us – who won't be able to hear the animals – think that you and Cathy are crazy, right?"

Heather giggles as she thinks about it. "So what are we going to tell the animals?"

"You and Cathy have to go to the zoo soon – like in the next couple of days – and talk to Joey the Baboon. He's been at the zoo for a long time and is on a special committee of animals that gets together after the zoo closes to problem solve or go over any issues that the animals are having. You will inform him that Cathy and her father will be visiting the zoo the following weekend and when they do, we want every animal to turn their back on Mr. Forsythe every time he and Cathy approaches an exhibit. We want every animal to ignore Mr. Forsythe and make it as obvious as they can that they are none too happy with him.

"Of course Cathy – who is on our side – will become whiney and dramatic, claiming the 'animals hate us because you're going to take away their land, daddy' and making sure the other visitors can hear and see what is going on. We'll have people posting pictures all over social media of Mr. Forsythe spending the day at the zoo looking at fannies."

Heather covers her mouth as she nearly explodes in laughter. "That is going to be so awesome!" she says before looking concerned, "Do you think it will work.? Mr. Forsythe is not an easy man to change."

"Are you kidding? God has given the same powers to all the animals in the community too. You know how much he loves his dog, Butch?"

Heather shakes her head in agreement.

"Cathy will be able to talk to him and get him to ignore his master every evening when he wants to go for a walk. Then Cathy will say, "I'll take him" and Butch will jump up wagging his tale and happily go for a walk with her. God can have every animal give Nick the silent treatment wherever he goes."

Heather can barely contain her excitement.

"By the time the city council gets together to vote on the property, we are hopeful that Mr. Forsythe will be there begging them to give the property to the zoo."

Heather perks up with enthusiasm, "That would be so awesome!" she says, trying to whisper as not to wake up the family.

"It will be a great victory for the planet. But first we have to get Cathy and you to the zoo."

Heather thinks for a moment, then perks up.

"Hey I know! One of the Cheetahs is pregnant and Cathy

loves Cheetahs. I could see if my Dad could take us tomorrow. He loves the zoo and seldom says no to a trip to the zoo."

"That would be great if we can do it tomorrow."

"But how do we talk to the Baboon with my Dad there?" asks Heather.

"Well your Dad has a good heart and we have just contacted his guardian angel to pay him a visit so he will understand what you two are up to and will understand that he is not to get in the way. I'm sure he'll be fine."

Heather thinks for a moment, then leans over and looks straight into the eyes of Marvin the guardian angel Monkey with a look of absolute determination.

"Let's do this! I'll call Cathy in the morning."

~~~~~~~~~~

"Hey Bill."

Bill Baker nearly falls over in the shower as the manly figure on his bottled soap container starts talking to him.

"Don't panic or do anything crazy. I'm your guardian angel and I need to talk to you."

Bill stands in the shower with water cascading over his body as he stares at the little man on his bottled soap talking to him.

"I know, I know, I know. This is not the ideal situation for me either, but I don't have a lot of time, and you are known for taking rather long showers, so I chose to talk with you here so we won't be disturbed."

Bill remains motionless in the shower just staring at the

cute little man on the bottle, as his guardian angel decides to keep moving as time is not on their side.

"Okay Bill, your daughter is going to ask you if you would take her and her friend Cathy to the zoo today and it's really, really important for you to say yes, okay?"

"Yes." says Bill who shows no sign of understanding.

"Good. Bill it is absolutely imperative that Cathy and Heather go to the zoo today, so I really need you to step up here, okay?"

"Okay. Who did you say you were?" Bill asks.

"Bill, work with me here. I'm your guardian angel and God has recruited your daughter and Cathy to do a very important assignment that requires them to be at the zoo today, so don't let us down, okay?"

"Okay."

"Good. And Bill, if you see Cathy and Heather talking to any of the animals, please don't question it, just turn and look the other way, got it?"

"Got it. I'm taking Heather and Cathy to the zoo today, because God wants them to talk to the animals according to my talking bottle of soap who is actually my guardian angel."

"Yes. Trust me Bill, it's going to be the start of something really big and you are going to be so happy that you didn't get in the way, I promise you that."

"Okay – Good to know."

"So you're going to the zoo today with Heather and Cathy and if by chance you see them talking to any of the animals you will turn away and just leave it alone, Okay?"

"Okay"

"I promise to come back later when I have more time to explain the assignment your daughter is doing, okay?"

"Okay"

"Do you have any questions?" his guardian angels says with a deep breath of hesitation.

"Just one."

The guardian angel braces, "Go ahead."

"Well that bottle of soap is almost empty and I was going to throw it away. Should I keep it until after you visit me again, or would you prefer another type of soap?"

The guardian angel stares at the earthling, not sure if he should burst out laughing or crying. "Whatever you want to do Bill, is fine with me. I'd be happy to talk to you in any way that makes you comfortable."

"Okay, good. So how do I get in touch with you?" he asks.

"I've been your guardian angel since the day you were born, Bill. We will stay in touch, my friend."

"Oh, okay."

"And thanks for helping out, Bill. God really appreciates you. It's going to be great, just don't screw it up."

As Bill gets out of the shower and is drying off, there is a knock on the door.

"Daddy, can you take Cathy and I to the zoo today, pretty please?"

Bill looks over to the bottle of soap as the cute little figure winks at him.

"Sounds good, honey. Give me a half hour to get ready."

3

A Trip To The Zoo

As Bill, Heather and Cathy approach the entrance to the zoo, Heather seems almost giddy because she is the only one, after all, that knows the assignment and what they are actually doing there.

Cathy enjoys going to the zoo, especially with friends. Being an only child who lives in a big mansion in the wealthy, private community outside of town, Cathy spends a lot of time alone. It's not like she has a neighborhood full of kids to play with. Her home IS the neighborhood, so Cathy spends a lot of time in her mansion alone playing with her imagination. Having this trip to the zoo with Heather is a welcomed break.

Bill is a good dad who works from home as a writer. He spends a lot of time sitting in front of his computer, so when Summer break comes and his daughter is home, he loves to take many breaks from his writing and be involved with his girl. Going to the zoo is one of his favorite activities, so this is a good day for him as he tries to comprehend how a bottle of soap was responsible for this outing.

As they get inside the zoo, Bill has always been good about letting his daughter dictate the agenda, and especially so this trip. He's not sure what exactly Heather is assigned to do, but he certainly got a clear message from his soap bottle that he was not to get in the way. Bill was going to simply go with the flow and enjoy the beautiful day.

Of course, first on the list of things to do was to go check out the Cheetahs as one of them is very pregnant and could deliver any day now. As they get to the exhibit, they find a sign that reads:

Mama Cheetah is in Delivery at our Hospital
with the best medical care available!
We Will Keep You Posted!!

Cathy and Heather are disappointed, yet excited. Especially Heather, who sees the perfect excuse for Cathy to get her father to bring her to the zoo this Saturday. She looks down at Marvin whom she grips uncomfortably tight in her arm and smiles with a whispered 'Perfect'.

As they head for another exhibit, Heather quietly lets Cathy in on her assignment and introduces her to Marvin her guardian angel Monkey. When Marvin smiles at Cathy and says 'Glad to meet you', Cathy stops with a shocked look on her face. She looks at Heather who smiles at her with assurance, then back at Marvin who is smiling and is very relieved that Heather no longer has a strangle hold on him, then back to Heather who holds a finger to her lips for quiet and whispers, "We have to go find Joey the Baboon and talk to him, okay?"

"We have to talk to Joey the Baboon?" Cathy asks.

"Yes. God wants kids like you and me to work with animals like Joey the Baboon in order to stop your dad from buying that property next door and let the zoo have it."

Cathy stops again, "Oh we're not going to stop my dad. He's pretty determined to get that development going. I know because I've tried, and he won't listen to me."

"I know, but now you have me, all the animals at the zoo and God on your side. I'm pretty sure your dad will change his mind." Heather says with confidence.

Cathy looks at Heather as her smile grows, "That'd be so Cool!"

Meanwhile, Bill is keeping a safe distance from the girls desperately avoiding listening to their conversation which, given the gestures and expressions, he thinks has something to do with the talking bottle of soap, so as much as he'd love to listen in, he thinks it best to avoid being too obvious and better preserve his sanity.

"Daddy, can we go see the Baboons?" asks Heather.

"Whatever you want, kiddo. To the Baboons!" he gestures pointing forward.

Cathy leans over to Heather and asks her about her Dad as Marvin jumps in.

"He's okay. His guardian angel visited him and told him he needed to take you to the zoo today and stay out of the way."

"But my dad doesn't have any stuffed animals." Heather says confused.

Marvin giggles, "I know. He had to take over a cute little man riding a horse on the bottle of soap while your dad was taking a shower this morning."

"My dad's guardian angel is a bottle of soap?" Heather laughs.

"Well, we angels have to take on a physical form in order to talk to our earthlings, and there wasn't much time, so his guardian angel had to take over the man riding a horse on the bottle of soap."

The girls get a charge out of that before Marvin continues.

"And trust me, he won't be doing that again. The other angels have been riding him hard in heaven, "Hey, aren't you that cute little man riding a horse on the bottle of soap?" Those angels will be laughing at that for a long time, I tell you that. Your dad will be fine, but I'm not so sure about his guardian angel."

They all laugh as Bill curiously considers what the girls are laughing about.

"Well here's the Baboons, girls." says Bill.

Heather and Cathy run up to the exhibit. They are glad to see that there are no other people at the exhibit.

"Do you think God is keeping the people away so we can talk to Joey?" asks Cathy.

They look around and have to admit that a lot of people are walking by at a safe distance and no one seems interested to check out the Baboons – one of the more popular exhibits at the zoo, one would think. Then they look at each other and shrug their shoulders.

"If so, we don't have much time, so we better get to work." says Heather as she looks at the Baboons and calls out, "Joey!… Joey, it's Heather and Cathy."

With that, Bill sees a concession stand next to the exhibit and tells the girls he's going to get a snack and sit while they look at the Baboons, as a big Baboon slowly makes his way towards the girls.

The Baboon smiles, "Which one of you is Heather?" he asks, as he was not facing them when she called.

Heather and Cathy look at each other in amazement that animals can talk. "I'm Heather and this is my friend Cathy." says Heather.

The Baboon smiles, "And I'm Joey. What can I do for you miss Heather?"

Heather looks down at Marvin who gives her an encouraging wink, before she responds.

"Well, God wants to save the planet and is going to use children and animals to lead the way."

Joey smiles, "Good move on Gods part. Adults over 30 seem to lose their ability to think, if you ask me. Go on."

"Well Cathy's dad wants to buy the property next to the zoo for development, but the zoo wants it to expand and build a medical research facility to help the animals, especially those that face extension, on the same property."

"I see." he looks to Cathy, "Did you tell your father what a bad idea he has?"

"Yes sir. But he won't listen to me. He has a lot of money and is use to getting what he wants." Cathy says with a tone of sadness.

Joey smiles, "Ah yes, money. Curios how the earthlings seem to think that the more money you have, the smarter you are. It's quite the opposite, you know. So how can I help?"

"Well Cathy is going to get her father to bring her to the zoo this Saturday to see the new Cheetah,"

Joey interrupts, "Ah yes, we just found out – it's a girl." he says with a big smile.

"Really?" asks an excited Cathy.

"Indeed. Good thing too. They need more females to reproduce and get their numbers going the other way. We're all very excited." says Joey.

Heather gets back to the plan, "So when Cathy is here with her father, we were thinking that maybe all the animals could ignore him when they approach each exhibit. You know, maybe turn your back on him and do nothing cute?"

Joey smiles, "I like it. We can call it the Full Moon Tour!"

Everyone laughs as Marvin gives Heather a high-five before Heather concludes. "So you'll get the animals to do this on Saturday, right? It's really important that all the animals participates because we plan to get pictures of animals ignoring Mr. Forsythe at the zoo and make them go viral so everyone can see it."

"You need not worry about the animals, miss Heather. I will call a meeting tonight and make sure that Mr. Forsythe gets a clear message on Saturday that the animal kingdom is not impressed with his plans." Joey looks to Cathy, "I apologize in advance to you, young Cathy, for our behavior on Saturday. We animals normally enjoy seeing the children, but I'm sure you understand."

"Oh yes, It'll be great. I plan to be whining at my father all day about how the animals hate us because of his stupid plan. I can't wait."

Joey smiles, "Ahhh whining children. The number one contributor to parents going mad. I love it. Whine away, young lady. Your father will be seeing nothing but fannies on Saturday!"

They all laugh as some children run up to the exhibit, letting Heather and Cathy know that it's time to move on. Joey winks at the girls and slowly makes his way back to the others as the girls reunite with Bill to finish their day at the zoo.

As they walk about the zoo, the mood is much more relaxed. Heather seems more engaged with her dad and the three really seem to enjoy the moment. As they reach the main entrance, having spent a full day exploring all the animals, they hear the announcement.

"Iiiiiit's a Girl! Please join your zoo in welcoming our new addition. A female Cheetah has just been delivered and both mom and child are doing well. Both mother and child will be in the nursery for public viewing on Saturday, so be sure to come by and say hello."

Heather and Cathy give each other an enthusiastic high five.

"I wouldn't mind coming back on Saturday if you girls want to see the new Cheetah." says Bill.

"I'm going to get my dad to take me. But maybe we'll see you there." says Cathy

"Great." says Bill, as Heather and Cathy giggle in celebration at how this day has worked out.

~~~~~~~~~

Meanwhile back at the CARPE DIEM Command Center, all the guardian angels are busy watching their monitors and following the progress, when suddenly an angel can be heard in a rather loud voice. "Hey soap boy, don't forget to get behind Bills ears on Saturday." As the room explodes into laughter, Bills guardian angel continues to look at his monitor, shaking his head and trying to ignore the laughter.

4

Joey Calls A Meeting

"Thanks for coming on short notice, but we have an issue that needs our response." says Joey to the gathering of zoo animals in the Rhino exhibit.

"Wait, who are you?"

"Leo the Lizard. I came instead of Tori the Turtle because it was such a short notice."

"Oh, right." says Joey, remembering how Tori often needs 2-3 days notice to get to their meetings.

"Okay, so everyone's here? Leo the Lizard for Tori, Ricky Rhino, Sal (the Elephant), Stanley Stork, Corey Cougar and myself. Great. I appreciate you all coming and if I may say so myself, I think you'll find this meeting to be a most entertaining.

"It has been brought to my attention that God wants to save planet earth and has recruited children to work with animals in order to save the planet. Any questions?"

"Joey, you always do that. Of course there are a million

questions. You just throw comments out there without explaining anything. Please continue." says Sal with a tone of aggravation.

"I know. I'm just mess'n with you." Joey says, tickled at himself, "But this is going to be so much fun and we're going to need everyone on board to make it work, so listen up."

Joey looks at everyone to make sure they are paying attention, which increases the annoyance they feel as they know how much Joey relishes being in the spot light.

"So what's the plan, Joey?" asks Cori Cougar, who is very impatient with Joey's leadership style and would prefer to have someone who gets right to the point and let the others discuss it.

"Okay, well I was talking to a couple of girls this morning…"

Stanley Stork interrupts, "Joey, Joey, Joey, please tell me you were NOT talking to the children! Are you trying to blow our cover here, or what?"

"No, no, no, Stanley, you've got it all wrong. The girls called out to me – by name- and I understood them. It seems that part of the plan God has is to give all of us in the animal kingdom the ability to understand the voice of a child and be able to communicate with them."

Joey pauses to let the others react.

"But what about the adults?" says Sal, "Every time we see children, they have adults with them."

"Well according to Heather – she's the girl who called me over – God thinks the problem with planet earth comes from the adults, so he wants us and the children to team up against the adults and turn this planet around."

"I'm in, I'm in, I'm in… let's do it!!" says a bouncing Leo who is a tad over anxious for the others who are use to Tori the Turtles mellow demeanor.

"Put the brakes on little handbag, we haven't even heard the plan yet." says Cori the Cougar as he looks to Joey.

"Well it seems the other girl with Heather, her name is Cathy, has a father who's got a lot of money and wants to buy the property next door to the zoo."

Stanley interrupts, "Hey isn't that the property where the zoo was going to expand and put in the research center?"

"Exactly! But Mr. Deep Pockets doesn't care about us and has more money, plus he owns the mayor and city council and he plans to have them re-zone the property for his shopping mall in two weeks."

The animals grumble is disgust.

"But Cathy really wants the property to go to the zoo, so she plans to bring her father to the zoo this Saturday because she wants to see the new Cheetah,"

All the animals join in comments of excitement at the new arrival.

" So anyway, Cathy wants us all to give her father a clear message that the animals are not impressed with his plans."

All the animals grumble in agreement.

"She wants every animal to turn their back on her father whenever they approach the exhibit. I call it the Full Moon Tour." Joey says with a great deal of self appreciation.

The others make a lot of approving small talk before Sal speaks up.

"So all we have to do is turn around and do nothing when we see this girl Cathy and her father come to our exhibit?"

"That's it. They want people to take pictures of all the animals ignoring Mr Rich Guy and make the photos go viral on social media.. By the time he's done at the zoo, he'll be having second thoughts about his fancy mall project – if we do a good job."

Ricky Rhino steps up, "I hate the humans. They've pushed my kind to the brink of extension for nothing but our horns. I'm going to tell my group to line up together, turn around and take a big dump for Mr Who-cares-about-animals Guy!"

The others burst out in laughter.

Stanley perks up, "Say, I could get all the birds who aren't caged to fly over and conveniently relieve themselves on mister fancy pants all day."

Again, the animals break into laughter and are rolling on the ground, high-fiving each other and enjoying the moment.

"Well hold on, fellas." says Joey with a serious tone, "We don't want Cathy's father to end up hating us – that would not help our cause. But maybe if some birds were to land on his shoulder and give him their cute little innocent looks, batting their eyes, rubbing their heads on his neck – you know the drill. Maybe he'd start to soften up a little."

They all mumble in approval.

"I'd be happy to land on his shoulder and give him my cute

innocent look." says Ricky as the others burst into laughter again.

"Oh Ricky, I love it, but we better stick to the Full Moon Poop in unison for you guys. That should give him a clear message."

"How will we know it is Cathy and her father?" asks Sal.

"I've got Stanley in charge of communications. I already talked to a Blue Crowned Conure who was in the tree next to the girls when we were talking, so she already knows what Cathy looks like. She's going to be at the entrance and when she sees Cathy, the birds will put in motion a messaging team of birds to keep us all aware of every step they take. If we do this right, it could be a huge victory for the zoo, so let's get the word out to all the others. And PLEASE remember – we don't want to make this guy hate us, we just want him to understand we are not impressed! Got it?"

They all mumble in agreement.

"Okay, you all know who you represent and we have three days to get the word out. Remember, 100% participation – no exceptions. Let's do it!"

~~~~~~~~~~

For the next two days, life at the zoo is abuzz with excitement. Not only the new addition in the Cheetah world, but word has been going around about the visit on Saturday by Nick Forsythe. All the animals are talking about the Full Moon Tour and having great fun coming up with ideas.

Joey has been frantically sending out messages to various groups to remind them of the seriousness of this mission and that even though their ideas are certainly cool, we must always remember that the goal is to get the property for the zoo and we must not jeopardize that goal.

Meanwhile, Cathy has been working overtime with her 'Daddy's Little Girl' title and plans to keep pushing it until her father agrees to take her on Saturday to see the new Cheetah, while God, who is following the progress of the experiment at Earth Operations Headquarters, could not be happier with the way things are falling into place.

One angel who has been following the progress, asks God if we might release the guardian angels of the city council to get them to the zoo on Saturday as well.

"Oh, certainly not. The plan calls for the children and animals to work together and they are doing a splendid job. We will not get any guardian angels of adults involved with this experiment unless absolutely necessary. I trust the children and animals. It's the adults that screw everything up."

Back at the zoo, Joey recruits the local Finch who likes to hang out at the zoo and was also in the tree next to Heather and Cathy, to go find Cathy and let her know there will be a Blue Crowned Conure at the front entrance Saturday and she needs to let the bird know they have arrived so the bird can send out the alert to all the animals.

The Finch flies away in search of the Forsythe residence. She asks many other birds, but nobody knows where they live. Finally, she runs into a sea gull who knows the family well.

"Oh yes, mister fancy pants lives right up the hill there

where all the highbrow live. Nice place. Great view of the ocean. 1450 Farthington Way. It even sounds snooty, don't you think?"

The little bird doesn't have time to chat, so she thanks the gull for the information and bolts towards the top of the hill.

When she gets over the security wall, she has no trouble finding 1450 Farthington Way, since there is clearly no 1448 nor 1452 anywhere in sight. The bird lands on a branch of a eucalyptus tree and surveys the property. Pretty big place. She figures she's going to have to just go window to window until she finds Cathy.

She starts at the top and goes window to window. What a spread. They have rooms everywhere. But finally, she comes to a window where she finds a little girl playing with dolls. She pecks on the window and calls for Cathy, who looks up and sees the bird. She gets up and goes to open the window.

"You Cathy Forsythe?" asks the bird.

"Why, yes I am. And who might you be?"

"I'm Oliver Finch. I'm just a local bird here. I just came from the zoo because Joey the Baboon wanted me to check on you."

"He did? Oh I love that Joey. I'm doing really well. It looks like my father is going to cave in on my nagging him to take me to the zoo Saturday, so I think it's going to work out. How's things at the zoo?"

"Oh Cathy, the animals are all excited about your visit Saturday and I think I'm going to get some of the locals to head over there as well. We don't want to miss the Full Moon Tour, as Joey is calling it."

Cathy giggles and quietly claps hers hands so as not to bring any attention from down stairs.

"Joey also wanted me to tell you that there's going to be a Blue Crowned Conure at the entrance. Her name is Alice. She was in the tree next to you when you were talking to Joey, so she's in charge of sending out the birds to alert all the exhibits that you guys are there. Joey's concerned that those Blue Crowned Conures are pretty stupid birds, so when you see her – she's bright blue and green – you are to tell your dad, "I think they're going to name the Cheetah Alice" and say it loud enough to get her attention. Then she'll know it's you and she'll take off and get everyone ready. I'll probably be in the tree as well, just as a back up plan, so nothing gets missed, Got it?"

"Got it. Oh this is going to be so much fun!" says Cathy dreamily.

"Okay then. I've got to go back and let Joey know we are all set for Saturday. Nice talking to you Cathy."

"Nice talking to you too. You're welcome to come by here any time if you want."

With that, Oliver flies off to the zoo as Cathy settles back with a big smile.

5

The Full Moon Tour

As everyone in Earth Operations settles in at the CARPE DIEM command center, the buzz is how God got a whole lot of whales and other sea animals to create a wild disruption just off the coast that caused an approaching storm to mysteriously change directions and harmlessly head back out to sea – which left a lot of coastal weathermen speechless trying to explain how the major storm they predicted for the weekend suddenly turned and went back out to sea, leaving the coast with a pleasant Saturday for a visit to the zoo.

God makes his way to a seat in the control booth so he can observe the trip to the zoo and see if their plan to save earth is going to be encouraged or discouraged on this day.

Everyone is excited and nervous at the same time.

Heather and her dad got to the zoo as soon as the gates opened. Bill's guardian angel payed him another visit, this time avoiding the embarrassment of his shower visit by visiting on his computer when Bill was looking for some clip art to support a story he was writing for raising kids. A cute Panda clip art was not ideal, but certainly much better than the bottle of soap. The guardian angel was able to have a much more detailed conversation with Bill about what the CARPE DIEM plan was all about and the guardian angel was very satisfied with how Bill not only understood the plan, but is more than happy to support the plan with Heather by writing some clever commentaries in support of the animals and the zoo.

Marvin the guardian angel Monkey let Heather know that her dad was well aware of what was going to happen at the zoo and she did not have to be cautious while she was with him.

All the animals at the zoo were excited about today. Joey made it clear that the animals were to behave normally for all the other guests as the impact will be far greater if the Full Moon Tour is only occurring in front of Mr. Forsythe.

Ricky went over the schedule for today with the other Rhinos and encouraged all of them to hold their poop until Mr. Forsythe approaches the exhibit and if possible to do it in unison, that would be great, but not to hurt themselves.

Alice has made her way to a lower branch of a tree right next to the ticket purchasing building so she has enough time to make sure it's actually Cathy and her dad while they are standing in line to buy tickets. The tree also has a good number of the local Finches, including Oliver, the one that spoke with Cathy, who are under strict orders to only observe the events of the day and not interfere unless absolutely necessary.

As Cathy and her dad get in line to buy their tickets, Nick is feeling pretty good. He knows he doesn't spend a lot of time with his daughter, so when he takes the opportunity to spend the day with her, it's always special for him.

Going to the zoo is not an issue for Nick. He likes animals and has donated to the zoo before. As a successful businessman, he is always clear that his business decisions are never personal, but strictly a matter of doing good business. The property next to the zoo is just one of the many projects he is working on and although he understands his plans will not be popular with zoo patrons, he also contends they will enjoy the nice restaurants and entertainment venues at the property. He has made the argument that the development will help the zoo, not hurt it.

As they buy their tickets and head inside, Alice overhears them talking about seeing the baby Cheetah that they may call Alice, so they head towards the nursery as Alice flies ahead to find a nice tree near the nursery while some of the Finches head out across the park to let everyone know the father is in the park. All the animals agreed not to have the Cheetah mother participate in the Full Moon Tour. They wanted the mother and child to have a normal day, and they also felt it was only right for Cathy to at least have this one moment to enjoy with her father.

"Isn't it precious, Daddy?" says Cathy when they finally get to the observation window. "Don't you just want to pick her up and hug her?"

Nick enjoys watching his daughter so full of enthusiasm, and is in no hurry to move on.

But Cathy is. She can't wait to see if the other animals can follow up with their ignoring behavior, so she tells her dad that she is ready to go look at the other animals.

The African Safari section is right next to the nursery, so Cathy wants to take her dad to go see the Rhinos, Elephants, Lions and others. Alice flies ahead to warn them that Nick and Cathy are heading their way.

The excitement in the African Safari section is very noticeable as the animals gather together towards the front. One of the Finches is on the back of Sal, the lead Elephant to help choreograph the moment.

"Okay, here she comes. See her over there holding her daddy's hand, coming right at us."

"About face!" says Sal the leader, as the elephants turn in unison and become unusually still.

"Hold it right there. Do not move a muscle until we get the all clear sign."

"What are they doing?" says one girl next to them.

"Is this part of a show?" says another.

"Mommy, why aren't they doing anything?" says yet another little girl.

Of course, this is only the first stop for Nick, so he doesn't make much of the fannie presentation as Cathy decides to stay quiet for now and simply let the animals have their say.

As they move on to the Lions exhibit, Cathy can hear the elephants blowing their horns in what sounds like a celebration as the visitors cheer their playfulness.

Nick of course is oblivious to the ruckus as he is simply enjoying his walk around the park with his daughter.

As they approach the lion exhibit, a Finch let's the lions know that they are coming.

"Okay, you kids come over here and remember what I told you – sit up straight, do not move or make any sound and just stare at this man with the adorable little girl."

Cathy, of course, can hear the lions talking and smiles at the mother lion as they approach.

Again, many of the other visitors seem a bit confused at the lions behavior. The young lions were running around chasing each other and suddenly ran over to their mother and are sitting perfectly still just staring out at the crowd.

"The animals don't seem very active today, honey. Guess we came at a bad time or something." says Nick.

"I don't know daddy. They were real playful the other day when Heather and I came to see them." says Cathy with a dramatic sigh and internal giggle.

"Well let's go look at the Rhinos, then. At least we can expect them to do nothing, right?" says Nick with a casual sense of humor.

The Finch on Rickys back lets him know they are approaching, so Ricky calls the others to take their places.

"It's about time. I don't think I could have held up on this poop much longer." says one of the rhinos as they all giggle and line up beside each other and turn around.

The Finch keeps them posted on what the humans are doing, and when Nick and Cathy get to the front of the exhibit, gives the signal.

"You are free to poop at will, fellas" says the Finch with glee as the rhinos begin to relieve themselves in front of an amused crowd of onlookers.

"Well at least they're doing something, right daddy?" Cathy says to her dad, "Maybe they are mad at you because you want to take away their property." she says to plant the seed to him for what's going on.

"Oh honey, animals don't think like that. They're too stupid to have any clue." says Nick, a bit humored at his daughters thought.

At that moment, Ricky lets out a very audible fart that makes the visitors laugh and gross out at the same time, while the other rhinos try desperately to keep their cool without bursting into laughter.

"Well let's move on." says Nick, and as he walks away, Ricky turns to Cathy and winks, as Cathy covers her mouth to hold back her laughter.

As the Full Moon Tour develops into a most entertaining day at the zoo, Cathy ramps up her whining with each exhibit in how the animals are mad at him for taking away their property. Even the visitors are starting to pick up on the action as they watch the animals playfully going about their day until this man shows up and they stop and do nothing, only to get playful again after he leaves. People are taking a lot of pictures and seem to be having a lot of fun watching this unfold.

Cathy decides to stop the whining as she doesn't want her dad to get mad at her and besides, the animals and people are doing more than enough without her.

When Cathy and Nick pass the Meerkats exhibit, the visitors are delighted at how every Meerkat stands up tall and in unison follow Nicks every movement with only their heads moving, making Nick a bit uncomfortable.

When they go into the Aviary to look at exotic birds. A Black Spotted Barbet lands on Nicks shoulder and sings to him in a very soft, gentle tone as all the other birds stand still on branches.

"Awwww, she likes you, daddy." says Cathy as she winks at the Barbet who then flies off, as Nick becomes even more anxious.

The Baboon exhibit decided to go with all the Baboons gathering around Joey and turn their backs on Nick, with only Joey facing him crunching down on a head of lettuce and glaring at him. The visitors found that really creepy.

Everywhere they went, Cathy and Nick were greeted by animals coming to an abrupt stop of their normal activities and just staring or turning their backs on Nick. People taking and posting pictures on social media of how the animals seem to be giving Nick Forsythe the cold shoulder treatment at the zoo.

By the time they work their way back to the main entrance, Nick is more than ready to head for the car.

As they head away from the zoo, Cathy and Nick are very quiet. Cathy is careful not to speak unless spoken to so as not to upset whatever chaos is going on in her dads head, while Nick seems to be numb with confusion at what just took place at their trip to the zoo.

Meanwhile, back at the zoo, the animals seem to be in a rather cheerful, playful mood as monkeys are flying from branch to branch and giving high-fives to each other as they pass. Even the Rhinos, who generally don't care much for the humans, seem to be much more animated with the visitors than would normally be expected.

All the care givers who work with the animals are noticing the positive energy going on throughout the zoo. It seems like the animals are all in a party mood today. They've never seen the zoo like this.

~~~~~~~~~~

"Get me the guardian angel for Nick." says God from his seat at the CARPE DIEM control center booth.

"Excuse me, sir?"

"Nicks guardian angel. I need to talk to him."

"Yes sir." says the angel at the controls as he holds a button down and calls out, "*Would the guardian angel of Nick Forsythe please come to the control booth.*"

An angel in the auditorium gets up, turns to look at the control booth in the back above the entrance, then makes his way to the back.

"I'm Nicks guardian angel, did you call me?" says the angel as he makes his way into the room.

"Yes, yes, come sit next to me." says God as the angel makes his way to the empty seat next to God.

"How is Nick doing?" asks God wanting the angels take on the situation.

"Well sir, I think he's a little taken back from the events at the zoo. I think Cathy was brilliant, though. She wasn't too heavy with her dad and did a beautiful job of backing off her whining and letting the animals and visitors create the moment."

God smiles, "I never have problems when I put kids in charge of an assignment. She was good, wasn't she?"

"Yes sir. I don't sense any anger from Nick. Anger would have made him more determined to take that property, so it was really important for Cathy to come through for us and she did a great job."

"You just can't go wrong with kids in charge. And the animals were perfect too. So here's what I need you to do." says God, "Nick has a pet dog, correct?"

"Yes sir . His name is Butch."

"Good. I want you to take over Butch and talk to Nick. I'll give Nick the ability to hear Butch talking."

"Okay. Do I tell him I'm his guardian angel?"

"Oh no. I want him to think his dog is talking to him. You can go back later and clear everything up with him after this is all over. The intent here is not to beat Nick but to win him over. If we beat him, there is going to be hard feelings and we don't want that. We want to win him over and let him see that this is just the beginning of a great movement to save planet Earth and if we get him to join us, he can play a huge role in helping us turn things around." God smiles.

The angel shakes his head with a big smile, "Nice. That would be great. So what do you want me to say to him?"

"Well to begin with, I know there is going to be a report on the evening news tonight about the strange behavior of the animals at the zoo. I'm going to have Heather be interviewed and after she speaks, I want you to say, 'Gee, I thought animals were too stupid to think. Seems they did a pretty good number on you today, right boss?' or something to that affect and just leave it there."

"Oh yeah, that will be awesome."

"Just be careful. I don't want you to make him think that everyone is ganging up on him. I want you to be 'mans best friend' to him and be the voice of reason with him. I don't need you to go crazy with it, just be that good friend that puts perspective on the events of the day. I have other ideas that will serve to get our friend Nick really questioning the choices he makes."

"That will be awesome. I'm all in. When do I start?"

"Go now before they get home and the evening news comes on."

With that, Nick's guardian angel disappears as God sits back with a big grin.

~~~~~~~~~~

In our community outreach segment, there was a lot of buzz at the zoo this morning and it wasn't from their new Cheetah that was born on Tuesday. It appears that businessman Nate Forsythe took his daughter to the zoo to see the newborn Cheetah and got a lot more than he expected. Our Jeremy Sounders explains.

Thanks Barbara.

I'm here at the zoo where visitors have been posting pictures all day on social media of what many are saying is a clear message to Mr. Forsythe from the animals.

To give you all perspective, you'll remember we've had many reports over the last several months regarding the property next to the zoo. The zoo has been working with the city for several years to purchase this property so they can expand the zoo and include a state of the art medical research building with a commitment to work with endangered species in a reproductive laboratory.

Of course, Mr. Forsythes company wants to buy the property and develop a large entertainment multiplex facility with restaurants, movie theaters and other projects. In order for him to do that, the city council will have to re-zone the property and that vote comes up next week at their meeting.

So that brings us to today. Mr. Forsythe, like many other parents, brought his daughter to see the new baby cheetah that was born last week and was being showcased at the nursery today for the first time.

The story is that as Mr. Forsythe and his daughter walked around the zoo, the animals would all stop and turn around or just stare at Mr. Forsythe without moving or making any sounds.

I know it sounds strange, but listen to some of the comments I got from those who were here.

"*We were watching the Meerkats running around and being cute as usual, when all of a sudden, they all stopped at once and stood up tall and just stared at this guy who was walking by with his daughter. said one visitor.*"

What happened afterwards?

"*Once he got by them, they went right back to their playing. We didn't know what to think of it.*"

I talked to a local girl who had her own ideas for the strange behavior.

"*It was so cool. Every time he approached an exhibit, the animals would stop what they were doing and turn their back on him. The animals knew that Mr. Forsythe was going to kill their expansion plans and they were letting him know that they were none too pleased about it.*" *(said Heather, whom Nick recognized as Cathy's friend.)*

And Barbara, I even spoke to one of the care givers at the zoo and listen to what she said.

Was that normal behavior for the animals today?

"*Well we have no control of the animals and we really try to create a normal habitat for each of them. There are times when the animals will be inactive. That's perfectly normal.*"

So you're saying this was perfectly normal, then?

"*Oh no. We've never seen behavior like this before – especially on this scale. I spoke with other care givers from other exhibits and it was the entire zoo. Every animal came to a stop when Mr. Forsythe approached their exhibit."*

Do you have any explanation for this?

"I really don't. We've never seen this before. It sure seems as if the animals were letting him know what they thought of his proposal for the property but we had nothing to do with it though."

I'll send it back to you Barbara with some of the pictures going viral on social media. These pictures say a lot, don't they?

They sure do Jeremy. says Barbara as the newscast returns to the studio.

The council will vote on the re-zoning issue on Thursday night at 6 and be open to the public .

Nick turns the TV off and looks to his dog, Butch.

"Come on Butch, let's take a walk. At least I can count on you to be my friend, right?"

"Oh I don't know. I thought we were all too stupid to think for ourselves?" says Butch, Nicks guardian angel dog.

'Well at least you're not stupid, pal." Nick freezes and turns back and looks at Butch. Then he looks around the room that is completely empty, then back at Butch.

"Oh, sorry boss, I forgot. We're all stupid AND we can't talk either. My bad." says Butch.

"Who are you?" asks Nick with a face full of fear.

"Well look who's stupid now. Can't even recognize his own loyal friend for the past seven years. Are we going for a walk or are you going to just stand there and stare at me all night?"

"But you're talking. Dogs aren't suppose to talk."

"I said I was sorry. But you were the one who said I was a friend you could count on. And from what I heard on that news report, you need a friend who can tell it like it is, my friend."

"But dogs don't talk."

"Oh, well you don't understand bark, so I decided to switch to your language so when I say you're an idiot, you'll understand me, okay?"

"I'm not an idiot!" says Nick in protest.

"Yeah, well looking at all the pictures that went viral of you watching a bunch of fannies at the zoo doesn't quite make you a genius, ya know."

"It's just a bad dream. Let's take a walk before I wake up." says Nick as he puts the collar on Butch and they head out the door.

Butch, the guardian angel dog plays it very cool, only responding to questions Nick has but careful not to say too much.

"So how do you plan to save me from the animal kingdom?" Nick asks as they settle into their normal walk around the estate.

"I didn't say I was going to save you, I told you as a friend that I would tell it like it is. Only you can save yourself from the animal fannies."

"Well a year from now, people will be enjoying some great food, movies and other entertainment and this will all be ancient history."

"Be careful my friend. I might remind you that it was you

who stated that the animals were too stupid. I'd hate to see you eating your own words later."

"I've been in business for many years, buddy boy, and I assure you that the people who are whining the loudest now will be the same people who stop me and thank me for bringing the great restaurants to their neighborhood. You'll see. Today was much about nothing."

"Well don't say I didn't warn you."

As they return home, Butch settles in to his normal sleeping spot as Nick heads up the stairs.

~~~~~~~~~~~

"How's it going with Nick?" asks God as Nicks guardian angel returns to the CARPE DIEM control center.

"I'm not sure. He just doesn't seem to get it." the angel says in frustration, "I've been around this guy for many years and I'm telling you, this is a heart that is hard to soften."

"Oh I wouldn't worry about it. Those hearts are often the ones that become my best ambassadors. He'll come around."

"So what do you want me to do tomorrow?" asks the angel.

God smiles, "Absolutely nothing. I want Butch to just be a normal dog tomorrow, unable to talk to Nick and just being a dog. Then the next day you can go back and talk to Nick some more. That boy will be so confused by Thursday, he won't know the difference between a dream and reality."

"I love it." says the angel as he sits back completely humored by the whole thing.

6

The Vote

As the Thursday vote approaches, there's a sense that everyone has done all they can to make their case about the property.

Heather and Cathy have become close friends. Cathy spent the night on Sunday and Monday they went back to the zoo again to thank all the animals for their help. All the animals were giddy about their role in the Full Moon Tour and encouraged the girls to let them know if they are needed for anything else.

Ricky Rhino came up to the girls and thanked them for the opportunity to make a statement, not just for the property issue, but for all the Rhinos and the abuse they have suffered.

Corey Cougar told the girls how hard it was for the cougars to lay there pretending to be asleep when they were giggling so much, until one of the cubs sneezed and he (Corey) turned his head and glared at Mr. Forsythe as if he caused the sneeze. It was just perfect timing and made their part a memorable one they will talk about for a long time.

The Meerkats were especially excited about their role on Saturday. They loved how they all stood at attention and just followed Mr. Forsythe with a blank stare, only moving their head. They laughed so hard after it was over, and they admit that some of the Meerkats still do it when a customer walks by without stopping to look at how cute they are. They'll stand up and stare as they walk by, then rush into their tunnels laughing out of control.

Joey had a nice visit with the girls as well. He said the animals felt that they made a big impact and were hopeful that the end result would enable the zoo to expand and get the much needed medical research center they so desperately needed. He encouraged the girls to come back often and that all the animals agreed that it's the children that make their life at the zoo so special.

For Nick, there was growing concern that the outcome may not be what the children and animals had hoped for. His company was expanding outside the city which means that Nick was out of town at the first of the week, so there was no opportunity for his guardian angel to take over as Butch, or the girls to work on his heart as the vote day approached.

Everyone at CARPE DIEM command center were concerned that in spite of their best efforts, the vote Thursday might not turn in their favor.

~~~~~~~~~~

Thursday morning finds Nick at the airport heading home

after three busy days out of the city getting contracts and overseeing some projects in other parts of the country. As is the norm for Nick, he only likes to be out of town for no more than three days a week, as being away from his wife and daughter any longer is too much for him. He always flies back to the city on an early flight on Thursday morning, drops by his office to get caught up with any issues within the company before heading home for an extended weekend.

As he was driving towards downtown, he noticed a For Sale sign on some retail property about a half mile from the zoo entrance. He was very familiar with the property as it was one of the many properties he was looking at before he settled on the larger property next to the zoo, so he didn't give it much thought.

As Nick pulls into his parking spot for his downtown office, he hears an announcement on the radio:

In local news, the city zoo announced that Joey the Baboon was found dead this morning. According to care givers, it appears that Joey died in his sleep of natural causes. Given his age and the treatment they have been giving him for heart issues common in older Baboons, they don't suspect anything out of the ordinary.

"He was being monitored for a heart problem that is common in older baboons. He was showing no signs of illness or anything in his behavior that would suggest anything other than age as the cause of death." reported the zoo veterinarian.

Joey was a favorite of local visitors and will be missed.

Nick sits in his car for a moment after hearing the news,

remembering how Joey just stared at him at the zoo a few days ago.

As he gets settled back in his high-rise office, Nick goes over everything with his administrative assistant and takes care of a few items that need his attention. As he wraps up his business dealings, he sits back and takes a moment to just look out his window at the city he has had such an impact on. He seems to be in no hurry, but then thinks about his wife and daughter and how much he'd rather go home to them than sitting here staring out the window.

When Nick walks into his home, he is greeted by his wife with a big hug. He is never rushed to end a hug with his wife as sometimes he feels she's the only real friend he has.

"Where's Cathy?" he asks.

"She's in her room. She's had a really bad day, so you might want to leave her be." says his wife.

Nick looks at her, "Joey?"

She nods in agreement, "She's pretty upset."

Nick makes his way to Cathy's room and finds her door open and she is lying on her bead face down with her arms crossed, holding her head up slightly. She has clearly cried herself to sleep.

Nick sits on the bed next to her and puts his hand on her shoulder.

"Cathy… Cathy." he says, trying to be gentle.

Cathy awakens and looks up to see her dad.

Nick looks at his daughter, "I'm really sorry about Joey,

honey." he says as Cathy wraps her arms around her dad and melts down with a waterfall of tears.

Nick is in no hurry to leave this moment. He finds himself in an unusual position. He has always been an unemotional businessman who understood the importance of a successful businessman never letting the emotional side get in the way of making good business decisions.

But this is his daughter holding him with emotional tears flowing out of her. He can feel his own eyes watering and simply wants to hold her without any words needed.

Cathy breaks the hug as she gets more control and apologizes to her dad.

"I'm sorry, daddy. It's just that Joey was such a special animal and it's just hard to imagine going to the zoo and not seeing him."

Nick wipes away the tears from his little girls face.

"Did I ever tell you about the time my dad took me to the zoo?" he says in a very soft tone that is unusual for him.

Cathy looks at her dad through watered eyes and shakes her head no.

Nick embraces his daughter again and holds her head to his chest as if to be whispering into her ear as he continues.

"I was young, around your age, I suppose, and I was so excited to have this day to spend with my dad at the zoo. He was a very busy man. A politician. He was always being called away from his private time to go deal with another crises, so going to the zoo with him was an exciting time, but I also understood it could easily be interrupted with yet another crises.

He pauses in thought, with tears weighing heavily in his eyes.

"Sure enough, we didn't get very far into our visit at the zoo before one of his body guards whispered in his ear. I knew that always meant something came up and we'd have to leave, and sure enough, my dad told me something really important had come up and we needed to leave right away.

"I was really disappointed because they had a new Baboon exhibit that I really wanted to see. But I had learned that there was no use in whining or making a scene. My dad was an important man and when the city needed him, there wasn't much I could do about it."

Nick holds his daughter up and looks into her eyes.

"All I really wanted to see was the Baboon exhibit. I loved the monkeys and was anxious to check out this new exhibit of Baboons. I never realized how much it affected me until I heard this morning about Joey."

As he looks at his daughter, tears begin to cascade over his eyelids. There is some sniffling back at the door, as Nick turns and sees his wife standing there overwhelmed with the emotion of the moment.

Nick looks back at his daughter, "I want you and your mother to come with me tonight to the council meeting."

Cathy looks a bit confused before her dad clarifies.

"I don't want to be the father my dad was to me." he says

as he pauses and a smile grows on his teary face, "I think you'll enjoy this meeting."

Cathy's eyebrows raise up as a smile slowly surfaces.

"Oh daddy!" as she embraces her dad with a very wet hug for both of them

~~~~~~~~~~

Back at the CARPE DIEM control booth, everyone is quiet and still as they watch the moment unfold. One of the angels at the control panel turns to God. "Was Joeys death your idea?" he asks with a smile.

God snaps his head to the angel and glares at him with a look that nobody would want from God.

"How dare you put me in the same category as the poachers! Do you honestly think I would kill Joey just to win Nicks heart? I will NEVER kill a living thing in order to win a heart. That will never happen!"

God pauses as he looks around at the fearful faces in the control booth, then smiles.

"I did make sure Nick saw that For Sale sign however. Making people see they have options is one thing I will do. Killing animals just to get my way is not. I didn't see Joeys death coming. I was just as surprised as the rest of you. I don't mess with the cycles of life."

~~~~~~~~~~

"The council recognizes Mr. Forsythe" says the head council member.

As Nick makes his way to the podium, there is much anticipation as to why he wanted to speak. The zoo administrators and legal team felt he had said enough and were pretty sure he was going to have his way tonight, so they felt he was grandstanding unnecessarily.

"Thank you, members of the council and guests. I wanted to take a few moments before your vote to submit a few minor changes to the plan."

Everyone sits back with a sigh, thinking that Nick has already won the property, so what else would he want?

Nick has never been one for long drawn-out speeches and prefers to get right to the point. "I would ask that the city council deny the re-zoning of this property in order for the Forsythe company to develop a commercial multiplex there."

"Excuse me?" says the head council member as everyone in the room sits up in disbelief of what they just heard.

"Yes, I would like to purchase the property as a private citizen and donate the property to the zoo for their expansion."

One of the council members interrupts, "Mr Forsythe, are you telling us you no longer want to develop that property? I'm dying to hear what brought about this change for your company." says the council member who has consistently been the voice against Nicks company.

"Well councilwoman, I realized this morning that I have options that the zoo doesn't have. There is another property on the same road about a half mile from the zoo. We looked at it initially but chose the zoo property because it was bigger and we could do more on the zoo property. I can revisit that property which is already zoned for commercial use and revise my plans to fit that property. On the other hand, if I continue with the property at the zoo, they would have no other options for expansion. As a businessman, I'm sure the council can understand that it is more beneficial for me to develop a commercial property on the smaller lot and benefit from having an expanding zoo with a thriving research medical facility a half mile away, than it is to develop the bigger property next to a zoo that has no hope of expansion. It just makes good business for me and the city."

Everyone sits back dumbfounded. This was not how they expected this meeting to go, and no one is sure what to do.

"Is there anything else, Mr Forsythe?" the head councilman asks.

"Yes. I would also like to offer my development team at my company to the zoo, free of charge, to help them develop a state-of-the-art facility. And I further want them to know that I will personally cover whatever shortfall their fund raiser is unable to collect, so they can proceed with their plans without hesitation."

Everyone looks at one another in disbelief.

"Is that all?" says the head council member.

"One more thing." Nick looks over to the zoo administrators, "I would ask the zoo to give serious consideration to naming the new facility 'The Joey'."

Members of the zoo cover their mouths as tears well up in their eyes. The CEO of the zoo looks at Nick, who is smiling at him. He tearfully stands up and begins to clap. Gradually, everyone is standing with an appreciative standing ovation. Cathy bolts to her father and jumps into a warm hug.

The head council member quickly wraps this up. "All in favor of keeping the property zoned for zoo expansion say 'aye'"

"AYE!"

"Those apposed" nothing, "Motion is passed. Meeting adjourned!"

The room breaks into an emotional celebration of hugs and tears.

Nobody saw this coming as the local media scrambled to cut into their programing with the news that the city zoo can move forward with their expansion.

As Nick and his family quickly make their way home, Nicks phone is buzzing out of control.

Local media desperately looking for an interview.

Business partners desperately seeking some clarity of what just happened.

But this was Nicks family night. As they got home, Nick turned his phone off and put it in a drawer as he fixed a couple glasses of wine and told Cathy to skip the bath time and join her parents out on the deck in the back.

The back deck was a huge place with lots of comfortable chairs and sofas, a big bar/kitchen/ bar-b-que and a big fire pit that was only used on special occasions.

This was a special occasion, as the Forsythes quietly sit around the fire pit watching the Sun set into the ocean in their million dollar view as a couple of Finches – which

Cathy recognized – softly entertained the family with joyous singing.

~~~~~~~~~~

Back at the CARPE DIEM control center, the angels have exploded into celebration at what has taken place.

God stands and asks the angel at the control panel for the microphone.

"Excuse me ... Angels ... Please..."

The angels quiet down and turn to the control booth.

"It's about winning hearts, angels. That's how we get our planet back. We have to win the hearts. Nice work, everyone. Now go ahead and celebrate!"

God hands the microphone back to the angel and walks out of the booth as the angels on the floor explode back into celebration.

7

The Plan Goes Public

"Ladies annnd Gentlemen. Please give a warm welcome to your very own creator.... the true author of love .... the one who put Earth on the map... your very own master of love-ins.... God Almighty!"

The Cloud Nine Assembly Hall explodes in celebration as the band amps up 'You Ain't Seen Nothin' Yet' and the party begins as God slowly makes his way to the podium. He's much more at ease this time around because everyone is completely blown away at how well the Heather experiment went and the optimism is higher than it's been in a long time at Earth Operations Headquarters.

Everyone is excited to get the CARPE DIEM plan world wide as so many of the guardian angels have been busy reviewing their own earthlings and how they can contribute to the plan. The ideas are dancing all around the building and gives God great energy and comfort that this plan is going to work.

God is in no way rushing the proceedings, but the band fully understands that everyone is anxious to get started, so they wrap up their music as the angels settle into their seats.

"Thank you all for being here." says God who pauses and smiles, "But I can't imagine any angel connected to Earth Operations was going to miss this celebration, right?"

The angels explode again in a celebration as the band breaks into a high-energy, rock'n 'Celebrate Good Times' with Joplin absolutely driving the song with her powerful, energetic vocals as the rest of the band tries to keep up. God steps back and lets the moment evolve.

After a good celebration, the angels and Joplin are ready to settle down and get to the business they are there for.

"For the last few weeks, earth time, we have all been watching the developments of our test run of the CARPE DIEM program, and I think you all would agree with me that the test not only passed, but it far exceeded what most of us were expecting."

A standing ovation, but this time the band holds off on turning it into a party.

"There are some important lessons we have learned with this test that I would like to point out before we go global with this program."

God hesitates and smiles and looks out over the crowded auditorium before he continues.

"And in case any of you had any doubts, let me be clear – WE ARE GOING GLOBAL WITH THE CARPE DIEM PLAN!"

Another eruption as Hendrix goes crazy on his guitar.

"But before we go global, let's understand what just happened. There are a few points to clear up and examine before we move forward.

"First, I want to be clear on one thing. I had nothing to do with Joey the Baboon's death. I give life, I do not take life away! It's bad enough that so many earthlings connect a death to some idea that I had a purpose in it. My purpose has always been, and will always be that earthlings live a loving life using their talents for the good of all and die of old age in their sleep. The same goes for my animals. My desire is always the natural cycle of life – much like Joey had. If I wanted to use death as part of my plan, I would certainly have not used Joey to get my way. I could just as easily brought death to the many fools who are making the decisions that has put Earth in danger. I do not use death, because if I gave a heart attack to the foolish who make the decisions, there will always be another fool around to take their place.

"Which brings me to my second point. This is NOT a competition. We are NOT looking to beat these people, we are looking to change their hearts. If we beat Nick in order to get the property, I would not be up here making plans to move forward, I promise you of that. Beating Nick would have caused hard feelings not only with Nick, but within his family and the community. Beating Nick would have been an empty victory that I would never support.

"We needed to change Nicks heart and move him to make a decision that was a benefit to all, and that is why we are celebrating now. We didn't beat Nick, we won his heart and he is now fully on board with us to help get Earth back on track."

A nice round of applause.

"This is critical if we are going to be successful. This is not a battle where there are winners and losers. The test was a success because there were no losers. Nicks business was a winner, as he develops on the new property to provide the community with the entertainment venues he promised them. The zoo was a winner, as they develop their new facility that will be critical in saving many endangered animals. The community wins because they have an awesome zoo to take their families to and wonderful entertainment venues to visit as well. This is absolutely the blueprint for us as we move to go global. We will not end a life in order to get our way, nor will we accept any losers in order to get our way. We only pursue winners and the only way to achieve that is through the heart.

"Our mission is not to save planet Earth. Our mission is to save the hearts that have let their love fade. Bring love back to those hearts and we will save the planet Earth.

"No losers …. Just Winners … that's the ONLY plan I will ever create!"

The angels explode into another round of celebration as the band drives out 'Nothin Gonna Stop Us Now' with Murray and Blaine pounding the rhythm, Harrison and Hendrix going crazy on guitar and Joplin just being Joplin on vocals. The Cloud Nine Assembly Hall is rocking! As the band breaks into a redundant anthem of 'All We Need is Love', all the angels wave and sing in unison as God claps along and takes it all in.

This is one party to be sure, but this band knows when it's time to settle, and so they do as God again steps up to the podium.

God smiles, "You know, if this all works out as we hope, I might consider turning those speakers and point them at Earth. Can you imagine everyone on the planet singing 'All We Need Is Love' and dancing in the streets?"

The angels explode with approval.

"But first let's get this plan going. I've made a few changes in reviewing our experiment. First, I am not going to give all animals the ability to speak and understand the voice of a child. There are many of my animal friends that have little contact with earthlings and I would not want to confuse them or get them off the path they are on. Instead, I am going to give all of you who will be at the center of these events the ability to give the animals the voice and understanding on an 'As Needed' basis. The animals are my friends, and I only want to include the animals in situations where they are needed. I will trust each of you to have a good understanding of your individual assignments and be able to make whatever decisions you need to help in your mission."

The angels applaud enthusiastically and give each other high fives.

"Next, I want each of you to give your earthling one of the two wristbands I just put on your arms."

The angels all look with surprise as they see the two wristbands appear on their arms.

"These wristbands will be the communication center for every child we have an assignment with. You will notice three colorful dots on them. The blue or pink one – depending on the gender you are working with – has a "G" on it. That will be their guardian angel contact button. I have given each of you the power to communicate with the animals involved as well as your earthling, but I don't think we need any more bottles of soap incidents."

God pauses as the angels bust out into laughter, as Bills guardian angel shakes his head in disgust.

"I want you all to have the flexibility in working your unique situations in the most advantageous way possible. If the situation warrants your being physically present with your child, by all means do whatever makes the child comfortable while working with you. Or you may want to simply visit your child every night to review the days events and plan your next step and then come back here to the CARPE DIEM command center and monitor the events from here, that's fine. The 'G' button will be your call button for the child to talk to you or come help them out. "The green button with an 'A' on it is for the animals. Once your child establishes a working relationship with an animal, that button will become their source of communication. There may be dangerous situations that we would want our children to be safe from, so that green 'A' button would be helpful, as the child could whisper in the ear of the animals while monitoring a developing situation. Again, we don't want this mission to take away any lives, so we obviously do not want to put our children in dangerous situations if we can possibly avoid it. The third brown button with a 'DOG' on it is only for you angels and is my own brilliant idea." God pauses with a smile before continuing, "This button is connected to a new division here at CARPE DIEM command center called the Department of Greed. I will have several earthlings who have already passed over to this side with a history of greed and selfishness that has left their hearts sadly lacking the love required to warrant an eternity in heaven. Any child who is working with a selfish, greedy adult and gets frustrated, you, as their guardian angel, are welcome to push the DOG button and be immediately connected to some of the worst offenders of greed and selfishness. I will personally oversee this department because I have hand picked each one with a clear message that I will be watching them very closely and would not hesitate to abort their participation and get them another assignment. I further assured them that if they mess up my children and animals any further than they have when they were alive, they will certainly not enjoy their next assignment." God pauses and smiles, "I'm confident you will find this button very useful for your work with the children, as you will be talking to people who fully understand how the foolish greed think."

"And before I let you all lose to get this program started, let me ask each of you to consider something for me. If and when we determine that this program has been a success and we find Earth moving in the direction that is beneficial to everyone, I would like to hear your ideas about moving forward. Do we go back to life as it was? Animals being animals, children being children with an assumption that the adults have learned their lesson and will truly continue down the path that benefits all? Do we continue with the animals and children continuing to be able to communicate with one another which potentially creates a new world of possibilities? Do we continue in a limited program that gives the animals and children the opportunity to respond to situations as needed? As I mentioned before, the goal is to change hearts. I am keenly aware that the program we are setting out with today will not only save the planet, but could have a profound affect on the planet moving forward. We want to make sure that we are all asking ourselves what measures should we take after we save the planet to keep the planet headed in the right direction and still provide a free will existence. It's going to need some serious thoughts and conversation and I ask you all to think about it as you work to save this planet."

God pauses before he wraps it up.

"I know that many of you who are guardians of children are anxious to get started and many already have a plan for your child. Those of you who are guardians of adults are anxious to begin monitoring your adults to find that window of opportunity to get them involved with this program as well. And of course for those guardian angels of the foolish few who have brought the planet to this point, you have the most important job of all. You must remember that we are NOT working to beat these people but win their hearts. You guardians must carefully monitor these hearts and continue to communicate with the control center to insure we are not doing anything that will make matters worse, and everything possible to soften those hearts."

God pauses again as he looks out at the angels.

"I trust my guardian angel Earth Operations program. I trust the children. I trust my beloved animals that have paid so dearly for the earthlings mistakes. I only have one remaining question for you all."

God pauses as he slowly grows a smile on his face.

"ARE YOU READY TO SAVE A PLANET?"

The angels explode in affirmation.

"LET'S TAKE BACK PLANET EARTH!"

The band breaks into, 'This Is Gonna Be The Best Day Of My Life' with thundering vocals and drums and builds with every angel dancing and singing along as this party cranks up.

God is in no hurry as he takes it all in. There is a lot of work to be done, but God knows you need to start with a coming out party to get everyone excited and motivated. And nobody does it better than Earth Operations. God will let this party go as long as they want and appreciates again how this side of his creation has no time values.

Party on, angels. Party on!

8

D.O.G. Central

"Excuse me God, but we have a new arrival for the DOG program." says the angel as God has instructed all angels to let him know when a good candidate for the DOG program arrives on this side, as he wants to deal with them personally.

"Excellent. Who do we have?" God asks.

"Mr. Charles Sodah"

"Really. He is one of the worst offenders. Glad he's off that planet." says God as he gets up to go retrieve his new addition to the program to the Department Of Greed.

God walks into the holding room where he sees Charles sitting there alone. God has been looking forward to getting Mr. Sodah on this side. He is the worst offender of the environment and human decency. He has no concern for how the products he produces affect the environment, or the employees who work for him. He makes several million dollars every week and is exceptional at buying politicians and law enforcement people in order to be left alone to his world of greed and selfishness.

"Mr. Sodah, welcome to my world. I'm God"

"I don't believe in God." says Charles, a bit hesitant.

"That is most unfortunate on this side Mr. Sodah, and I assure you that your money and power means nothing over here either. Your political influence means nothing to me. I judge people's life by the content of their hearts, not their bank accounts or power, and frankly Mr. Sodah, after reviewing your heart, I'm not impressed. But don't worry, I can fix that, so follow me."

God starts walking down a hall, as Charles looks around, slowly gets up and walks out the door with a great deal of hesitancy.

"You know, on this side time is like your money – it has no value here. Because it is eternity, I can certainly take whatever time I need with you, but of course, you know the old saying, 'If you surround yourself with idiots, you'll become an idiot' or something like that. So I'm sure you would understand I don't want to spend too much time with you."

As God stops at a door, he opens it and looks at Charles, "Please, come have a seat."

They enter a dark room that looks very much like a movie theater, which of course it actually is. But instead of movies from Hollywood, this feature is all about Charles.

As they settle in without any conversation, the movie begins.

It's not a long movie, it's more a slide show of the faces

that have been touched by Mr. Sodah's life of greed. The young mothers who works 60 hours a week in foreign sweat shops and still sends their children to bed hungry most nights. The politician who started out with so much promise yet compromised his good character in the name of payoffs that has made him a wealthy man and not a leader for the good of the people. It's just a sample of the many lives affected by Charles. There are many more stories to be told, but God knows hearts, and when he sees a heart that understands the consequences of the choices made, there is no need to continue.

As the lights go up, Charles looks at God, not with a look of horror, but more a resolved look that you'd expect from a man who is use to only seeing what he wants to see.

"I'm going to hell, I suppose?"

God looks at him, "There's no hell. Why would I ever create a hell?"

"You mean there's no devil?"

God looks at Charles with a strong dose of irony.

"You believe in the devil, but not in me? A good example of how money doesn't make a person smart. Again, why would I create a devil? So people like you could blame the devil for the poor choices you made in life? I create love. There is no hell. There is no devil. You were created in my image and that image is a foundation of love with the capacity to grow and contribute to the world around you. You were also created with a free will. I wanted the earthlings to be able to make choices and create a path of life as they wish without me interfering all the time."

God pauses to let Charles consider it before he continues.

"You and you alone made the choices that denied the love you were created with to grow. The devil didn't make those choices. I don't want to hear about your parents, your 5th grade teacher, or anyone else. You chose to turn away from love.

"I gave you a life with a solid foundation of love and a capacity to grow that love as you wish." God points to the screen that shows a sweat shop with many tired, hungry sad faces struggling to survive, "And this is what you brought me in return. Now you consider yourself a pretty smart businessman, Mr. Sodah, you tell me – would you say I got a good return on my investment?"

Charles stares at the screen, then looks over to God who is waiting for a response.

"What is to become of me, then?"

God snaps his fingers and a live camera shot replaces the sweat shop scene. It appears to be a business with lots of uninspired cubicles with high walls around what appears to be earthlings, sitting with head phones on while watching their monitors.

"See that empty cubicle to the left? That's all yours. You have just joined the Department Of Greed which is an affiliate of the CARPE DIEM Plan that I have created in an attempt to save planet Earth from people like you.

"The CARPE DIEM plan involves the children and

animals of the world working together to save the planet before it's too late. These children may have to deal with foolish adults who make a lot of money and buy a lot of power to continue to make even more money with no concern as to how it affects the rest of the world. You and all those people you see sitting down there are experts at greed. I have instructed my guardian angels assigned to children to let the children know they are welcome to call the DOG – that includes you – at any time for advice and strategies in working with these adults. Both the children and the guardian angels will be able to contact you for advice as needed."

Charles shakes his head with a pained look, "I really don't do children well. Isn't there something else?"

God looks at Charles, "Well, Mr. Sodah, your life reflects a resume that suggests that you didn't do ANYTHING well except greed. That seat is the perfect place for you on this side because your only passion was greed, and being the Department Of Greed, who better to answer the hot lines than someone like you? I have no doubt that you'll be great because, if I may say so, no one did greed better than you."

Charles starts to sink in his seat, thinking he may have been better off burning in the eternal pits of hell than doing this job.

"Let me be clear, Charles. Children and animals are the best things I created for earth. I would strongly encourage you to seize this opportunity to help the children out as they save the planet. If you screw up with any of my children, I assure you that I have other assignments for you and trust me, they will not be assignments of pleasure for you."

Charles looks at the DOG call center then at God as God wraps up.

"Your wealth is no good over on this side Charles, and I have all the power. I have many assignments that I could give you that would have you begging me to create a fiery pit of hell for you. I create love and I plan to get your heart back to that foundation of love I originally gave you so you can proceed. You would be smart to make good use of this opportunity, Mr. Sodah."

God looks at Charles and let's the moment sink in for him.

"I'm really not good at talking to children." says Charles matter of factly.

"Well that's probably why you became the foolish man that you did. Children are great to talk to. Why, I could use up a whole lot of eternity just talking to kids. They are so innocent with such a positive energy. As far as I'm concerned, I gave you a great assignment and I'm confident that you will be thanking me later."

He looks at Charles with a more serious tone.

"Here's the bottom line, Mr. Sodah. I AM God, whether you believe it or not, and I have every bit of faith that you will eventually come around to my world built from love. It may not be the DOG program. It may be two or three assignments down the road. I never lose a heart, Charles. I don't plan to lose yours. That's why I made this side eternity. I'm a patient God and I'll do whatever it takes to win a heart."

God pauses as he sees that there is nothing more for this moment.

"Go take your seat and help the kids out." God says as he disappears and leaves Charles alone with an angel.

"If you'll follow me, I'll show you to year seat Mr. Sodah."

The angel leads Charles to the empty cubical, "Here's your seat. Good luck."

Charles panics as the angel starts to walk away, "Wait a minute. Don't I get any training?"

The angel stops and turns around and comes back to Charles.

"No. Sit down and help the kids."

"But I've never done anything like this before. Surely you have a training program."

The angel looks at Charles with a cold expression, "I believe they have a saying in your world, 'Treat others the way you would want to be treated', right? How much training did you give those poor people working in your sweat shops?"

"But…"

The angel interrupts, "Listen, I have a lot more interesting things to do than talk with you. Besides, your lights blinking. You have a call you need to take. Be nice to the children."

With that, the angel disappears, leaving Charles alone at his cubical. He looks around and all the others are busy talking in their cubical. Slowly he sits down in his chair. He sees the instructions on the wall;

Put Headset On

Press Blinking Light

Be Nice to the Children

Mr Sodah is full of fear. He's never done anything like this before. He hesitates, but knows he has no other choice, and reaches for the blinking button.

"Hello"

With that, the Department Of Greed welcomes what God hopes to become one of the best workers for the CARPE DIEM program.

9

Amahle and Peter Parrot

God goes back to his world of creating new worlds. He wants to give the CARPE DIEM program some time to develop, and will check in from time to time to see how things are going, but for now, he's busy creating.

Amahle is the daughter of a Ranger in South Africa. Her dad, Khayone, works in the Kruger National Park with his primary responsibility being to catch the poachers who are killing primarily the Rhinos but other animals as well. It's a frustrating job as the poachers always seem to slip away and be one step ahead of the authorities. He spends most days finding the dead carcasses of various animals, not the ones responsible.

Amahle loves her dad and what he does to save the Rhinos and other animals. She loves the animals of South Africa and doesn't understand why anyone would want to hurt them. Especially the Rhinos. Her dad has explained the reason the poachers are killing the Rhinos, but Amahle doesn't understand how they could kill the Rhino just because they want their horns.

Amahle spends her days playing around their humble home just outside the Crocodile Bridge Gate of the park where her dad works. Her mother spends the days doing chores and visiting neighbors, so Amahle is left alone with her imagination and many stuffed animals her dad likes to bring her from the places he goes. She almost has every animal from the park in her collection and loves to pretend that she is a worker like her dad saving all the animals.

One day as she was playing outside with her animals, her stuffed Giraffe calls out to her.

"Amahle, don't be afraid." says the giraffe as Amahle sits back on the ground and stares at her stuffed giraffe who is now walking towards her.

"I'm your guardian angel and I was sent to you because God needs your help." says the giraffe as it gets up to Amahle's knee.

Amahle doesn't know if she's dreaming or what.

"My guardian angel is a giraffe?" she says as much a statement as a question.

"No, Amahle, I'm an angel, but in order to talk with you, I need to take on a physical presence, so I chose the giraffe because they have longer necks and I won't have to yell at you."

"Okay. And God needs my help?" she asks in a tone of uncertainty.

"Yes. God has created a plan that will help your father out in his work." says the guardian angel giraffe.

"Then why don't you talk to my dad?"

"Because the program is for children and animals only, so it has to be you who does it."

"Does what?"

"Save the planet. God is giving the animals the ability to talk to children and understand the voice of a child, so the animals want to talk with you and help your dad find the poachers so they'll stop the killing."

Amahle perks up, "That would be so cool. What animal do I have to talk to?"

"They'll come to you. I just wanted you to understand what was happening so when a bird starts talking to you, you won't panic because you'll understand, got it?"

"Got it. So what do I tell my dad?"

"Well Amahle, God doesn't want you telling lies, of course, so just tell your dad the truth – that a bird is telling you where the poachers are hiding out and where they are going the next day. Your dad may not understand at first, he may never understand his daughter talking to animals, actually, but you just have to convince him to try and see. Once he sees how well it works, he's not going to question you talking to any animals you want to, I assure you that."

Amahle shrugs her shoulders unconvinced, "Okay, if you say so. So when do we start?"

"There is a brown headed parrot in the tree in your back yard that is waiting for you. I told him to wait until I explained the program to you, so you wouldn't be afraid. Amahle, it's important that you listen and follow through with whatever the birds tell you in order for our plan to work, got it?"

"Got it. So, what's the parrots name?"

"Parrots don't have names Amahle. You can call him whatever you want."

Amahle brightens, "Really? I think I'll call him Peter – Peter Parrot – isn't that cute?"

"Adorable. Just be sure and do whatever – Peter – tells you."

"Okay. By the way, what is your name?" Amahle asks curiously.

"Angels don't have names. I'm Amahle's guardian angel, that's all."

"I'll call you spot!" says Amahle with firm conviction.

The giraffe looks up at her and shakes its head, "Dogs are named Spot."

"I know, and very few dogs have spots. Isn't that silly? But all giraffes have spots, so I'll call you spot, okay?"

The angel shakes his head in displeasure, "Whatever you want, Amahle. As long as the program works and the poachers are stopped, you can call me Spot."

"YAY!" says the excited girl, then stops, "Are you going to be in my giraffe all the time now?"

"No. I'll be back at Earth Operations watching how this plan is working out. But the wrist band you are wearing is a communication bracelet. If you push the pink button, you can talk to me. If you push the green button, you can talk to Peter. And the button with a dog on it is not going to be used much for this assignment as it's for children who are working with adults and need some counsel.

Amahle looks at her wrist and is puzzled as to how it got on her wrist, and looks at Spot.

"I'm an angel, remember. There's a lot of things I can do that you may find a bit confusing, but just go with it for now, got it?"

"Got it. So when I want to talk with you, I just have to push the pink button and yell Spot!?"

"No, that won't be necessary, Amahle. No yelling Spot, just calmly talk to me. Keep in mind that I'm connected to your heart, so I'll always know what you are feeling and will show up in the giraffe when it's needed."

"Okay. Can I go now and find Peter?" says the anxious girl.

"Yes, but take the giraffe with you in case you need me."

"Okay, Spot. Thanks for coming by." says the little girl as she runs off to the back yard and Spot heads back to the CARPE DIEM Command Center at Earth Operations Headquarters, where he is immediately hounded by fellow angels for his name.

"Welcome back, Spotty!"

"Hey, Spot, if you have a girl are you going to name her Dot?"

"Dot 'n Spot!"

The room fills with laughter as Spot desperately tries to

ignore the angels as he watches his monitor to see how the plan is working with Amahle and Peter.

"Peter .…. Peter Parrot are you here?" yells Amahle into her wrist band as she pushes the green button and reaches the back yard where there are many trees.

"Girl, stop screaming. People might think you're crazy."

Amahle looks over to the tree where Peter is perched on a lower branch, slightly hidden by leaves.

"Are you Peter, the one who's going to tell me how to catch the poachers?"

"Well I'm the one who's going to tell you how to catch the poachers, girl, but I'll have you know I'm one fine female parrot and I do not appreciate being called Peter." says the parrot with a tone of attitude.

"Oh, sorry. Spot said the animals don't have names, so I'm calling you Peter Parrot – isn't it cute?"

Peter stares at Amahle while she wrestles with the merits of pursuing the issue of naming her such an unglamorous name, or to simply let it go in the name of stopping the poachers.

"Spot?" asks the parrot.

"Yes. My guardian angel took over my giraffe here, and they don't have names either, so I called him Spot."

Peter looks at the giraffe and then at Amahle, "Well, at least you didn't call me 'Feathers' I suppose."

Amahle giggles, "No. Feathers Parrot doesn't sound very good at all. I like Peter Parrot better."

"Well if it gets the poachers out, honey, you can call me whatever you want."

"So how are we going to catch the poachers?"

"I have got a network of birds working together ever since we heard about the CARPE DIEM plan,"

Amahle interrupts. "Excuse me – Carpe Diem plan?"

Peter stares at the girl, "Didn't Spot explain Gods plan to you?"

"Oh, Gods plan. He just said the animals can speak and understand children and that's how we're going to save the planet."

"I see. Maybe the name was appropriate after all." says the female Peter as Amahle giggles. "Gods plan is called the CARPE DIEM plan which means – Children and Animals Rescue Planet Earth by Disarming the Idiots and Empowering the Many. We – the animals and children of the world – are the many, while the adults – for the most part – are the idiots." Peter pauses to let this sink in for Amahle.

"My dad isn't an idiot!" she protests.

"I know, Amahle, but of all the living creatures on this planet, the human adults are the only ones who actually choose to become idiots. And ironically, it's those idiots who are making the decisions that are killing the planet for everyone. Your dad is a good man and hopefully, we can help him get rid of some of those idiots."

"That'd be great. What do you want me to do?"

"As I was say'n, I have put together a network of birds that are following the poachers and listening in on their plans – God gave us animals the ability to hear the conversations of the adults, but we can't communicate with them because he doesn't want a lot of cursing. So when you hear me sing like this," Peter chirps a specific cadence, "you will know that I have information. You'll come out here and then you can give your dad the information and together, we can stop the poachers."

"Cool. Do you have any information for my dad now? He's at work right now, but sometimes comes home for lunch."

"No. My birds are out there investigating and listening in on the poachers to better understand how they work. You stay close and I'll be back as soon as I get some information that will help your dad, okay?"

"Okay, Peter. This is going to be fun to stop all those bad people from killing the animals."

For the rest of the morning, Amahle stayed close to her back yard paying close attention to the tree that Peter would come to with information. It seemed to Amahle to be the longest day of her life.

Then, in the late afternoon, Peter shows up on the branch of the tree and sings her song for Amahle, who saw her coming and was already bolting towards the tree.

"Peter, I'm here. Did you find anything out?" said Amahle out of breath slightly.

Peter needs a second, as she still has a problem hearing the name Peter when she is called when she knows she is such a fine young lady bird, but the assignment is too important to get worked up about that now, so she moves on.

"Oh girl, are you ready to see your dad become a hero?"

"He already is, but where do you want me to send him?" says Amahle with great enthusiasm.

"Okay, listen carefully. You know where the Nianganzwani lookout is?'

"Yes, I've been there a lot with my dad."

"Okay, tell your dad to go north of that lookout about two and a half kilometers, just east of the Nthahdanyathi Hide. There's some Rhinos around there and the poachers are going to camp out at the Hide and go after a Rhino just before sunrise, got it?"

"Got it! Thanks, Peter, I'll make sure daddy gets there before the Sun."

"Okay girl. Tell your dad to be safe. Those poachers have no respect for life of any kind you know."

"I will. Thanks again Peter." says Amahle as she heads inside.

That evening as Khayone tucks his daughter into bed, she tells her dad about the CARPE DIEM plan that God has started and how Peter, the female brown headed parrot, let her know where he can catch the poachers.

Khayone looked at it as his daughters wonderful imagination, yet at the same time, she was so convincing and serious, so before he went to bed, he thought it might be worth getting up early to check out her story. He contacted a few other Rangers and told them to meet him at the Nainganzwani lookout at 4am.

Early the next morning, Amahne is awakened by the call of Peters song in the back yard. As Amahle gets her bearings,

Peters song gets louder and more desperate. Amahle senses that something is wrong, so she sneaks out to the back to find Peter.

"Girl listen up. There's a situation we weren't ready for. One of the Rangers in your dad's group works for the poachers. He's been tipping off the poachers and that's why your dad can never catch them."

"You mean my dad didn't get them?" Amahle says with a sad tone.

"I'm sorry, girl. Your dad will find nothing when he gets there. The good news is that the poachers were going to get the Rhino ahead of your dad, but a bunch of us birds got into their faces and annoyed them enough until they decided to just leave."

"Well I guess that's a good thing anyway." says the dejected Amahle.

"Yes, it's good that we saved the Rhino, of course, but we didn't stop the poaching. We need to refocus our plan and help your dad get the informant locked up. We animals were not aware that humans would behave like that, but now we understand. It's not enough to just tell your dad where the poachers are, we have to make sure that no one is tipping the poachers off."

Amahle looks at Peter a bit frustrated, "But how can I convince my dad when our first message didn't work out?"

Peter stands up straight, "Girl, we animals don't take kindly to human idiots making us look bad. Now that God has given us the ability to listen and understand human conversations, we are all moving forward with putting an end to this senseless killing…. and girl, we have a LOT of birds alone out there working the assignment. After only one night, I can tell you the name of the informant. I can tell you that he told his wife to go to the specific bank and make a deposit this morning. I can tell you that the banker at said bank is also on the take and will gladly put her money – less his cut of course – into the special account that is 'untraceable'. And that's just the birds, Amahle. I had to do some work this morning to keep the other animals from going after the poachers. With the ability to hear and understand what the poachers are planning, I think it's safe to say that the poachers have poached their last horn," she says with great attitude, "But we made it very clear to all the animals that the goal is to change the hearts of humans, and we can not do that if we start killing the poachers. In the animal world, we only kill for food, and let me tell you girl, there is not one animal on this planet that wants that piece of meat. No offense, child, but you human taste awful."

Amahle takes it all in, but is still concerned about her dad. "So what can I do to get my dad to believe me?"

"You can tell him the truth, girl. You can tell him that he didn't find the poachers because he has an informant in his group who tipped them off. You can tell him that the informants wife made a nice deposit at a local bank this morning and that the banker is also on the take and won't show you any of the 'special' accounts they have set up for the informants. And you can further tell him that if he pays attention to the information we give you, he will not only solve the informant in his group, but he'll be cracking the network of informants throughout the region and putting a lot of informants and bankers in jail for a long time."

"But I'm not sure my dad will listen to me after this morning." says a dejected Amahle.

"Listen, Amahle, the goal is to stop the poaching, and now that we have the ability to listen and understand the humans, we animals can stop the poaching without any help from the humans. Your dad may blow you off today. That's okay. But I assure you Amahle, I will come back every day and give you more information for your dad. You will tell him what I tell you. I assure you eventually, maybe a week or maybe a month, your dad will start paying attention because he will be seeing the results of what I tell you. Your dad's a good man, Amahle. I'm sure it won't be long before your dad comes home from work and asks you what the birds are telling you."

Amahle smiles, "I hope so."

"I know so. Amahle, it's important to the animals that we break this poaching ring without killing anyone. We want to change the human hearts, so we feel strongly that we must do so not just by stopping the poachers, but by doing so without harming any humans. We want the humans to understand that the animals want to live in peace and will always only kill for food, never anger."

Peter pauses to give Amahle a moment to think about it.

"Listen, Amahle, I know your dad will come home today frustrated and probably not willing to listen to you again.

That's okay. He loves the animals and wants so badly to stop the poachers and that's where is anger and frustration lies, Amahle. Don't argue with him. Understand that his anger and frustration isn't with you. Be gentle and tell him what I've told you. The animals didn't know about the informants and that's why he failed this morning. But encourage him that now that the animals understand this, they are going to do everything in their power to help him put an end to the informants while the animals stop the poachers through our networking. Tell him to pay attention to how the animals are behaving. Pay attention to the poachers. He's going to realize very soon that what you are telling him is true. We all want the same thing Amahle."

"Well, I guess it's good that no one got killed today."

"Exactly. Your dad has a good heart. He'll come around. You just keep coming to me when I call and give him our latest information. And always tell your dad to pay attention to the animals he loves so much. He's going to see."

"Okay Peter. I'm sorry it didn't work out today."

"Girl, it worked out great for the animals – remind your dad that at least he didn't find a dead Rhino." Peter looks at Amahle to make sure she is paying attention, "And Amahle, your dad will NEVER again find a dead Rhino as long as God gives us the ability to listen to the conversations. Every day when your dad comes home, I want you to ask him how many dead animals he saw from poaching. Keep track of how many days he says 'none'. Eventually, he'll understand. The animals will stop the poachers, and your dad can stop the informants. We will win, Amahle, we will win!"

Amahle smiles as she starts back to her house, "Okay, Peter. Thanks. I'll make sure daddy gets the message. See you later." as she runs into her home.

~~~~~~~~~~

Back at the CARPE DIEM Command Center of Earth Operations Headquarters, God has dropped in to check on the progress. He sits in the control booth that oversees the main floor where the guardian angels are busy monitoring their part of the program. Some of the cubicles are empty as the angels frequently visit their earthlings when needed.

"So how are things going on Earth?" says God in a jovial manner, "Should I start throwing rocks?" he says with a smile.

"No rocks, sir. The program is doing well. Some areas better than others, but in all areas we are making progress." says the angel at the control panel.

"What area is doing best?" asks God with excited interest.

The angel doesn't have to think about it, "Well the poaching issue is pretty much a done deal. Once you gave the animals the ability to listen and understand the human conversations, they pretty much took matters into their own hands. They've been frustrating the poachers to a point where many are giving up."

"But no violence, right? We solve the problem with hearts of love. No violence." says God emphatically.

"No violence, sir. The birds are following the poachers and listening to their conversations and passing on the information to the animals in danger. Every time the poachers show up at a location, there's no animals except birds in the trees laughing and singing. It's created a lot of distrust among the poaching community as they feel like someone is tipping off the animals, which doesn't make sense to them, but it's created quite a bit of confusion. The bottom line is that there hasn't been one killing on planet Earth since the program started, and the children are helping the friendly adults break up the poaching rings, so the poachers are getting it from both ends and many are simply giving up. They're not making any money and they are seeing many of their friends being arrested and doing hard time, so most of them are simply giving up."

"Excellent. Just remember, we want to change hearts. We want all the earthlings to understand that killing these animals so other people can have cute little trinkets or some belief that they are being cured of some ailment is never okay. I don't want to just stop the poaching, I want to make it so people don't even consider it."

God sits back and smiles, "I knew getting the children and animals involved was going to work. And let me be clear – I am in no hurry to take away the animals ability to listen and understand the conversations of humans. I want to see at least a full generation without poaching before I even consider removing that from the animals." God pauses and smiles again, "You know I did say that the earthlings were in charge of planet Earth, and that they needed to be good stewards to all living things on the planet. But I never said I wouldn't give the animals the ability to encourage them to make better decisions, right? As long as the earthlings put the idiots in charge, I'm certainly open to keeping the animals able to counter those decisions."

God looks out over the room full of busy guardian angels before he continues.

"How about the other areas of concern?"

"Well sir, the rain forest issue seems to be going well. The difference between the poachers and the rain forest is that the poachers are killing with really no justification – they do it for trinkets. But the rain forest issue has at least a mild justification in that they argue they need the land for farming and grazing livestock. We can stop them from cutting down the rain forests, but it's going to take a little longer to develop and work out the long term of need between atmosphere to breath and food to eat and sustain life."

"And food is one of the issues too, right?" God asks

"Yes, and that's where we can combine our efforts in this program. It's not enough to simply stop cutting down the rain forests. We must be able to develop new technologies and opportunities that makes it possible to leave the rain forests alone and let them regenerate and improve the environment. We can stop them from cutting down the rain forests, just as we stopped the poachers. But in the case of the rain forests, we have to give them a better option for their food supply before we can succeed."

"And the water issues?" God asks.

"That's going to take time to clean up the oceans and

develop better water management, but that mostly involves science and development. We have ideas in development which look very promising, but it will take time to really see if the ideas can work out."

"So overall, we can feel optimistic that the CARPE DIEM program is going to succeed?"

"Oh, yes sir. Like you mentioned before, there aren't that many bad earthlings making bad decisions. Once the animals and children start making progress, we are finding a lot of the adults getting behind them and working with them to make these changes a long term reality."

God stands up to leave, being satisfied with the report, "I knew it! Putting the animals and children in charge was the right thing to do. There's a lot of good hearts on that planet. We just needed the children and animals to give the adults a nudge to stand up to the idiots and say no more." says God as he makes his way to the door. Before he exits, he turns to the angel at the control panel, "You know, I've been developing an idea of creating a planet with nothing but animals and children. I've got a few kinks to work out yet, but I'm thinking that would be a pretty nice paradise."

With that, God goes back to his creating.

~~~~~~~~~~

A lot of what Peter told Amahle in their initial meeting has come to be true. Khayone was at first cool to his daughter after the first failed attempt to stop the poachers, but during the ensuing several weeks, he's noticed the changes that his daughter told him would happen.

He hasn't received any reports of animals killings.

He's noticed the animals are a lot more relaxed and accommodating to those who are working to protect their environment.

Even the media is starting to take notice, reporting the unusual decline of poaching events and how there seems to be an unexplained reversal of poachers being frustrated because not only can they not locate the animals, but they are seeing more and more of the informant rings that was frustrating the authorities, now being dismantled with informants and bankers going to jail.

Amahle has been consistent in her conversations with her dad. She always starts by asking him if he found any dead animals – just to remind him that she told him the animals were not going to let them kill any more. She also lets him know any information that Peter gives her, which he is starting to take seriously as he was able to bust the informant in his group and stop the ring of corruption in Kruger National Park.

As Khayone tucks his daughter into bed, he asks her about this Peter she's been talking to. She tells him everything, of course, as she remembers that God doesn't want her to lie.

"Why can't the animals talk to me?" asks Khayone, trying to understand.

"Because God was afraid that if the animals could talk to the adults, they might get too emotional and start cursing a lot, so he decided to stay with animals and children only." Amahle says with a big smile.

Khayone laughs out loud, "That God must be one smart cookie, right?"

"Well, I guess that's part of being God" says Amahle.

"Listen, Amahle, I am sorry I doubted you when you first told me about Peter Parrot. But I have come to realize that you were not only being truthful, but you were trying to help me do my job. I could never thank you enough for being such a good daughter." he smiles as he reaches into his jacket pocket and pulls out a stuffed Brown Headed Parrot and hands it to her.

Amahle takes the parrot and gives her dad a big, embracing hug. "Oh thank you daddy! Where did you find it?"

Khayone smiles, "I looked everywhere for that. All the gift shops in the park. Finally, I found it in a bird exhibit at the museum of nature in the city. I was so excited."

Amahle gives her dad another hug, "It's perfect daddy! I love it!!"

Khayone holds his daughter and looks into her eyes, "I'd like to go with you the next time you talk to Peter, okay? I know she can't talk to me, but I want to be there when you tell her how much we appreciate what the animals have done."

"Okay, daddy."

The next day Khayone was off. He was working from home and doing some chores to help his wife. When Amahle heard Peter's call, she grabbed her stuffed parrot, called out to her dad and made her way towards the back yard.

Her dad joins her at the tree where Peter was waiting.

"Look Peter at what my dad got me! I'm calling it junior, kinda after you."

Peter looks at the stuffed animal, then at Khayone, then at Amahle, "How sweet."

"My dad wanted to come with me today so he could meet you and say thank you." says Amahle.

Peter looks at Khayone, who doesn't hesitate.

"I wanted to say thank you Peter, to you and the other animals for making my job a joy again. You have stopped the killing that I have been trying to stop for years and for that, I am truly grateful. For the first time, I am able to go to work and do what I always wanted to do – make sure my animals are safe and living well."

Peter looks at Khayone with a deep sense of compassion, then to Amahle, "Tell your dad he has a good heart and all the animals appreciate what he does. Tell him we will do whatever we can to help him do his job and to not be afraid if some of the animals approach him in the park – they come in peace to say thank you."

Amahle tells her dad, who looks at Peter with a nod of respect.

"I'm so sorry for all the animals we have lost. I wish I could have stopped the killing. I have spent many nights crying tears of sadness for how they've treated you." he says with humility.

"Tell your dad we have cried with him." then Peter looks to Khayone, "And tell him from now on, only tears of joy."

~~~~~~~~~~

A report from the World Animal Protection Agency shows a dramatic decline in poaching world wide. The agency reports that there have been no killings of endangered animals in the past several weeks and at the same time, there has been an increase in the number of reports of poaching rings being busted with several arrests of key figures in the poaching black market.

The WAPA has no explanation for this dramatic turn around in the areas greatly affected by the poaching black market.

Harold Ragan reports from South Africa:

Thanks Judy. In talking to the people on the front line of the poaching issues, they have no explanation for the turn of events. They tell me there is no inside information that is contributing to this positive outcome and can only tell us that for some reason, the animals are avoiding the poachers.

I asked a ranger at Kruger National Park about the positive reports.

Tell me Khayone, you've been on the front lines here at Kruger National Park for several years trying to stop the poachers. Can you explain what has changed recently to apparently stop the killing?

"I believe God just got tired of the humans senseless killing of animals so he gave the animals the ability to avoid the poachers."

So you're saying it's an act of God then?

"Absolutely. God has given the animals the ability to understand the poachers conversations, so the birds are following them and then reporting to the other animals so they can get out of harms way."

I see. And how do you explain the many reports of the poaching rings and the black market being busted? Do the birds tell you that too?

"Well, I'm not at liberty to explain how we are getting an upper hand on the poachers, but I can assure you that the animals have been a great help to us. We are very thankful to the animals."

Okay Judy, there you have it. It appears that the only explanation for all this good news is that God has given the animals the ability to eavesdrop on the poachers and are passing along their information to all the animals involved. So I guess we all need to be careful what we are saying around our cats and dogs, right?

Back to you Judy.

~~~~~~~~~~

God suddenly appears in the control booth at CARPE DIEM Command Center.

"Who's that reporter?" God says anxiously.

"Ummm, Harold …. Harold Ragan, sir" says the angel at the control panel.

"Does he have a cat or dog?"

"Ummmm… no sir …. Oh, but he does have a parakeet, sir."

God sits back and smiles, "Oh, does he now…. Get me his guardian angel right now!"

"Would the guardian angel for Harold Ragan please report to the control booth immediately."

"So, I guess we'll have to be careful about what we say around our cats and dogs, he says? Time to have a little fun with this program, fellas." Says God with a devilish grin.

10

Bonnies Bricks

"Eduardo" calls the Toucan from the open window of his bedroom.

Eduardo is the son of a very important government official in charge of regulating and issuing licenses for deforestation of the Brazilian rain forests. His dad, Francisco, fully understands the issues facing deforestation and the reduction of the rain forests and works hard to look for solutions that will benefit both sides of the debate.

Francisco has a good heart and is in a good position within the government to make some changes. He is aware that the most important concern about deforestation is that without an alternative solution to the needs of agriculture and livestock, the deforestation will continue to endanger the rain forests that is so important to the health of our atmosphere.

You can't just stop the deforestation on a moral platform of protecting our atmosphere because they will counter the moral platform with the argument that people need food as much as they need to breath.

Francisco works diligently to balance the needs of both sides as he constantly looks for solutions that will provide the food needed in a growing world without destroying the rain forests needed to provide a healthy atmosphere for the same people in need.

"Eduardo, get up buddy, we need to talk."

Eduardo sits up in his bed and rubs his eyes, shakes the cobwebs out of his head and wearily looks around his room to see who it is speaking to him.

"Hey Eddie boy, it's me over here on the window sill. Don't be alarmed, I'm your guardian angel and I have a great project for you to work on."

"My guardian angel is a Toucan?" says the young boy still half asleep.

"Well for now, I am. You see, as an angel, I have to take on a physical form in order to talk with you, so I chose to be this awesome Toucan because I love to fly and I think the colors of a Toucan makes me look totally awesome."

The angel looks over to Eduardo who is just sitting on his bed staring at him with an expression that suggest he's trying to figure out if this is a dream or if the Toucan is actually talking to him.

The Toucan flies over to Eduardo's pillow and raises his wings to smack Eduardo on either side of his face repeatedly to get his attention.

"Come on, buddy, wake up now. This isn't a dream and

we have a lot to talk about. Are you with me, Eddie boy, are you with me?"

Eduardo smacks the bird, who goes rolling off the bed as the boy protests.

"What kind of guardian angel are you coming here in the middle of the night to smack me like that. I'm just a kid you know."

The Toucan shakes his head clear from the boy's walloping before he flies up to the night stand next to the bed and perches there – safely out of reach of the boy.

"I'm sorry about that Eddie boy, but I really do have to talk to you and it's important that you pay attention."

"What's so important that you have to wake me up like this?" asks Eduardo.

"It's a new program that God has developed to save planet Earth and you'd be a great help to the program."

"But I'm just a kid. What does he need me for?"

"Because the program is for the children and animals of the planet, and you qualify because you're a kid."

"Children and animals? What do we have to do?"

"Change the hearts of the adults who are screwing up the planet."

Eduardo stares at the Toucan as if to be thinking, then shakes his head.

"That's a lot of hearts."

"I know Eddie boy, but who better to change those hearts than the children and animals of the world, right?"

Eduardo continues to look at the bird in thought.

"No one's ever called me Eddie boy before."

"Oh, well, does that offend you?"

Eduardo looks away in thought, shaking his head in negative motion., then looks back at the bird.

"No. Just say'n, that's all."

"Okay. Well,…"

Eduardo interrupts the bird, "What's your name?" he asks.

"I'm an angel. We don't have names. I'm simply Eduardo's guardian angel." says the bird anxious to move on.

"Oh."

But before the bird can say another word, Eduardo continues, "Do you want a name?"

"It doesn't matter. You are the only one who can hear me or talk to me, so it doesn't matter." says the bird desperately ready to move on.

"Well I think it matters to me. I like to have the name of a person I'm talking to."

"That's fine. You can name me whatever you want, but we really do need to go over the program."

"How about Bob? That's an easy name to remember. Do you want to be Bob?"

"That'd be great kid. From now on I'll be Bob."

" Okay. So, what can I do for you Bobbie boy?" says the boy with a smile.

Bob stares at the sarcasm before he moves on, "Yes, well… God needs the children and animals to work together to save the planet, so he gave all the animals the ability to listen and understand a child's voice and be able to talk to them."

"The animals can talk to me?" says Eduardo with a tone of excitement.

"Yes. That's the only way the animals and children can work together to save the planet."

"Cool. So what do they want to say to me?"

Bob seems to relax as it appears that Eduardo is finally ready to hear the plan.

"Well, you're dad has been working hard to find a way to stop the deforestation of the rain forests, but to do so, he has to find a solution to the food issues that are causing the deforestation, right?"

"Yea, I think he gets really frustrated because both sides make good arguments." says Eduardo, who thinks of his dad as a hero for the work he is doing to solve this problem.

"Exactly. You have to have an alternative solution for the food before you can stop the deforestation."

"So do the animals have the solution?" Eduardo asks curiously.

"Well the animals don't, but now that they can talk to the children, they will be able to help the children get the solutions already available into the focus of the world."

"So the solution is already out there?" asks Eduardo.

"It's not just one solution, Eddie boy, it's a whole slew of solutions that are out there. The problem is that the people in charge – the adults – aren't paying attention, so those solutions are not getting enough support. We just need the kids and animals to work together and force the adults to pay attention by putting these solutions in motion."

"Wow, that sounds cool. How do we do that?"

"I'm going to get a group of animals from the rain forests to gather nearby tomorrow night, and I need you to get your dad to come to the meeting. I'll be back here tomorrow afternoon and will lead you to where the animals are meeting. I'll explain the whole program to you, your dad and all the animals gathered. We will all have assignments when we leave that will put the program in motion. The main thing right now is for you to get your dad to join us at the meeting tomorrow."

"Well that won't be easy. What do I say to my dad?"

"Tell him the truth. He won't believe you, of course, but your dad has a good heart and he really wants to find a solution to this problem, so it's important for you to explain to him that as crazy as this all sounds, he needs to trust you and go along. Once he's there, I think your dad is going to get really excited, so do whatever you can to get him to come, okay?"

"I'll try."

~~~~~~~~~~

God enters the control booth at the CARPE DIEM Command Center.

"Get me the guardian angel for Francisco."

"Will the guardian angel for Francisco please report to the control booth immediately." says the angel in the microphone at the control panel.

"Did you call for me?" asks an angel who steps into the booth.

"Ah, yes," says God as he stands and offers the angel a seat next to him, "You're the guardian angel for Francisco, Eduardo's dad, right?"

"Yes sir." says the angel as he takes his seat.

"Tell me about Francisco. He has a good heart I understand."

"Yes sir. He's a good man who works very hard to preserve the planet." reports the angel.

"Yes, yes. And do you feel he'd be a good addition to our CARPE DIEM program?"

"Well, yes sir. He's in a good position to get things done and his heart is very sincere. I think he'd be a lot of help to our program."

"Excellent. That's what I was thinking as well. I want you to visit him. I want you to be a migratory bird and I want you to explain to him the CARPE DIEM Plan so that when his son approaches him about this meeting, he will understand and not delay the moment."

"Yes sir, but a migratory bird?"

"Yes. I have a young girl in California, in the USA, who has the gift that will create the solution, so I need a migratory bird who can take the meeting of the rain forest and deliver the message to this girl who has the solution and with your help can get this solution moving."

"Okay. I'd be happy to do that. Now is Francisco going to have the same abilities as the children? Will he be able to talk with the animals at this meeting or will we use Eduardo to serve as a translator?"

"No. Francisco will have the same abilities as the children, as long as you feel his heart is sincere. He and Eduardo can work together at there end while you head to California to work with Bonnie and together we can start connecting the dots that will provide the solutions we need."

"Yes sir. You mentioned a Bonnie?"

"Oh Yes. That's the girls name that you will be talking to. She's a very compassionate girl who loves the ocean and lives in San Diego in California. Her dad is an engineer who has the skills to develop the solutions to our issues with the rain forest. I need you to take notes at the meeting that Bob is having with Francisco, Eduardo and the animals and then go find Bonnie who already has the solution. She can develop that solution with your help and I'll talk to Bonnie's guardian angel as well to get her on board too. Her dad will take note and create the process that will take that solution to a much greater level."

"Brilliant as usual, sir." says Francisco's angel.

"Well, let's not get ahead of ourselves. This is a free will environment that I have created, so it's never a slam dunk."

"Yes sir. Anything else?"

"No. Just be optimistic. There are a lot of solutions there on Earth. We just have to get them out of the obituaries and onto the front page."

"Yes sir. I'll pay a visit to Francisco right away."

"Be positive. The children and animals are going to do great things for planet Earth."

~~~~~~~~~~

"Francisco ….. pssst… Fracisco." says the guardian angel bird.

Francisco bolts up and looks at the small bird standing on his chest, then looks over to his wife who remains sleeping.

"Francisco. I am your guardian angel. Your wife can not hear me, only you. So be quiet because if you start talking, your wife will wake up, I'll fly away, and she'll think you are a lunatic, okay?"

Francisco shakes his head and stares at the bird.

"Francisco, I have to take on a physical presence in order to speak with you because, as I say, I am your guardian angel. Please do not be alarmed and listen to what I say, okay?"

Francisco looks at the bird, then over to his wife who is in a deep sleep, then back to the bird.

"Go on." he says with great hesitation.

"Good. Eduardo is going to talk to you in the morning about a meeting he wants you to go with him to .You are not going to understand anything he says about this meeting but I strongly suggest that you simply agree to go with him and do NOT give him any grief about it, Okay?"

Francisco stares at the bird for a minute before saying, "Okay."

The bird walks up and gets right into Francisco's face.

"It's really, really important for you to go to this meeting Francisco. And it's even more important that you simply say yes and not ask your son a bunch of questions. The meeting will explain everything. You just need to be at that meeting, you understand?"

Francisco just stares at the bird, then looks over to his wife who is still sound asleep, then back at the bird.

"Oooookay." says Francisco with great hesitancy.

"Great. I'll be at the meeting as well, so if I land on your shoulder, don't panic and brush me off – I'm there to tell you something. Otherwise, just pay attention to the meeting and help your son out – and the rest of the world, got it?"

"Got it." says a bewildered Francisco.

The angel takes his wings and holds Francisco's face in a loving manner, "You're a good man Francisco. This is going to be a good time for you, I promise you that. But for now, go back to sleep." says the bird before it flies out the window and into the night singing.

~~~~~~~~~~

"Thanks for coming everyone." says Bob who is perched on a stump of a fallen tree. Eduardo and Francisco have put their lanterns by the stump so everyone can see.

"To start with, I wanted to give you each a name because Eduardo here likes to have names connected to those he is talking with, so I have given it great thought and come up with names for each of you." he pauses to make sure they are paying attention. "Okay" he steps over to the green anaconda and says, "You will be called Snake," he goes over to the Jaguar, "you will be Jaggie," then to the spider monkey, "you are Spider," and then to the howler monkey, "You will be Howler." he gets back on the stump and stands very proud of himself, "And of course, my name will be Bob." he pauses, then looks to Eduardo, "Is that good enough for you Eddie boy?"

Eduardo shrugs his shoulders, "Not very creative." he says matter of factly, as the animals seem to agree with Eduardo as the steam of pride fizzles from Bob's chest.

"Hold on now." says Bob in protest, "Remember, I'm an angel and we don't have names in heaven. Besides, this meeting is not about naming the animals, so if we can kindly move on I'd appreciate it."

Snake says, "Okay Bob. Why aren't you named Bird, or were you named Bob because you always bob around when you're nervous?" he says as the other animals laugh.

"Ha ….. Ha….. Ha ….. "says the unimpressed Bob, "Eduardo named me Bob and I didn't make fun of him, so you all can just take the name I gave you and move on with the more important issues we are gathered for, alright?"

"Okay Bob." says all the animals in unison followed by great laughter.

Francisco leans over to his son, "I didn't realize the animals had such a sense of humor." he whispers as Eduardo shrugs his shoulders and smiles at his dad.

"I also added Fracicso's guardian angel bird over here because he will play an important role in our plans." says Bob anxious to move on, but bracing himself for the obvious.

""What's his name – Bird?" yells out Howler as the others start laughing again and agreeing on the name.

"Bird, Bird, Bird" they all say in unison as they role around in laughter.

Bob hangs his head in humility as 'Bird' glares over to Bob.

"Okay, okay ... please, can we just start this meeting?" says Bob as the others settle back down. He looks over to 'bird' and asks, "In the interest of time, are you okay being Bird?" says Bob.

"It looks like I have no choice. It's usually the earthling that you work for that names you though."

Bob turns to Francisco, "Are you okay with Bird?"

Francisco is surprised to find the focus on him and is startled, but responds, "Of course. It's not really a name, but certainly consistent for this group, I suppose."

The animals all laugh again.

Bob waits in disgust as the others take great pleasure in the manner that this meeting has started. But they do realize that there is more to this meeting than names, so they collect themselves and give their attention back to Bob.

"I will remind everyone here that on this side time matters, so if we could get serious now, we have a lot of plans we need to develop." says Bob as the others seem ready to move on.

~~~~~~~~~~

Back at the CARPE DIEM Command Center, God comes into the control booth to get an update.

"How are we doing on Earth, fellas?" asks God as he makes his way to a seat.

"Well, the poaching seems to be a dead issue now,"

God interrupts, "I know. That's why we're working on it." God says

"Excuse me?" says the serious angel at the control panel who turns to look at God.

God smiles, "You just can't let a play on words get past you, ya know. A dead issue – I know, that's why we're working on it – That's a good one. I'm happy the dead is on the issue and not the animals, to be sure. Go on."

"Yes sir. Well the rain forest issue is developing nicely. The animals of the rain forest are meeting now and after the meeting, Bird," the angel turns to God, "That's what they named the guardian angel of Francisco."

God laughs out loud. "Bird? Okay let's review. Since this program started, we have a Spot a Bob and a Bird., right?"

The angel adds, "We also had a female Peter the Parrot, sir"

God is greatly humored, "Well I'm certainly happy to know that the success of this program is not dependent on good name selections." he says as everyone in the room agrees in humorous harmony.

"Yes, so anyway, Bird is going to California to work with Bonnie on the brick project as soon as the meeting of the rain forest animals concludes."

"Okay, get me Bonnie's guardian angel." says God as the angel at the control panel turns to his microphone.

"Would the guardian angel for Bonnie please report to the control booth."

As God waits for the guardian angel, he shakes his head, "Bird. That's not a name, that's an identity."

"Well sir, it does goes with the other names of the group. There's Snake, Spider, Howler and Jaggie." says the angel.

"Who gave them those names?" asks God.

"Bob, sir. Eduardo's guardian angel. He was quite proud of his cleverness."

God shakes his head, "I created the angels to be on a practical level of thought, as I wanted the earthlings to be the creative thinkers. I guess this program confirms that I did a good job with that, right?" God is again humored as he turns to an angel observing in the back, "That Bob is one clever angel, isn't he?"

"Did you call for me?" says Bonnie's guardian angel as she walks in the booth.

God stands up and moves over one seat and offers the other seat to the angel.

"Yes, please come in. Thanks for coming." God says as the angel makes her way to the seat and they all sit down.

"I need you to work with Bonnie on this brick program that I need to get up and running as soon as possible." says God as he pauses in thought, "But before we do that, let's get a name for you beforehand. There seems to be some confusion on what a good name is down there, so if you and I can nip that in the bud, we can save a lot of time down there."

"Okay." says the angel

"Let's see, I wanted you to be a Pelican while you're working with Bonnie because they are awesome flyers and with that big bill, you can help with the clean up of the ocean. It'll be a nice fit for you to be bringing her the trash of the ocean while working with her without causing a lot of concern from other earthlings."

"Okay. I'd like to fly – and over the ocean would be great." says the excited angel.

"Good. Now a name." God thinks, "You are going to be instructing Bonnie on the brick program, so how about Polly the Professor?"

"Polly the Professor. That sounds very dignified, sir." says the angel.

"Well it sounds a lot better than Bird." says God as the room fills with laughter.

"Okay, so Polly, I have created this program that will turn a lot of the garbage the earthlings are dumping in the ocean into bricks that can be used to build farms upwards and leave the rain forests alone. It's an easy solution that a child can do, which is exactly the point of CARPE DIEM. Once you get Bonnie going on this program, her father – who is a brilliant engineer wasting his time at a company creating worthless products that people don't need – hopefully, he will embrace the idea and help his daughter on a much bigger scale. This is vital to the planets survival. The solutions are there, but we have to get those solutions on a much greater scale if they are going to be successful."

"Sounds good. How do I get this program?" says Polly the Professor.

"Once you take over a pelican, I'll have it programed into the brain, so you'll be one smart bird!" God says with a smile.

"Excellent. I know Bonnie is going to be a great help to this program. She's got a really good heart. We won't let you down, sir."

"Well don't sound so dramatic. That's why I chose Bonnie. She's a great kid and I know she's going to do fine. And if we have to get her father's guardian angel involved, we can do that too." God pauses as he looks at Polly, "I'm not throwing rocks at this place. We're going to win and you and Bonnie are going to be an important part of this victory, okay?"

"Yes sir. This is going to be exciting. When do I start?"

"Well there is a great ocean breeze blowing in San Diego right now and you have a lot of bricks we need to start making. Tell Bonnie I appreciate what she's doing for us, alright?"

"Will do. Thank you sir."

As Polly makes her way out of the booth and into the Pacific Ocean, God sits back with a content smile.

"Okay, from now on I want the guardian angels to have names. I want every guardian angel of a newborn child to report to an angel name caller so we can look at the environment of the child and come up with a proper name, okay?"

God shakes his head, "Snake, Spider, Howler. Jaggie and Bird …. Bob, Bob, Bob. I shoulda saw that coming, I guess."

God gets up to leave, "Okay, let me know if you need me for anything. I have to go find an angel for the name calling job. It's looking good so far though… name calling excluded of course."

~~~~~~~~~~

Bonnie is in her back yard playing in her sandbox as she is prone to do on a pleasant summer day in San Diego. She loves digging and building in her sandbox and has many dolls and stuffed animals with her to help her solve the problems of the world in her imagination.

Suddenly, a pelican lands on the edge of her sandbox and dumps a bunch of trash in her sandbox from her mouth.

"Hey, what are you doing? Get outta here you crazy bird." says Bonnie as she tries to brush the bird away. Polly avoids her swing and perches again on the side of the sandbox.

"Hold on Bonnie. I'm not here to mess up your game, I'm your guardian angel, okay?"

"My guardian angel is a pelican?" asks Bonnie not very convinced.

"Well, as a guardian angel, I have to take on a physical form in order to be able to speak with you, so I am a pelican. My name is Polly the Professor."

Bonnie looks at the pelican with great uncertainty.

"My guardian angel is a professor and a pelican?" she asks curiously.

"Yes. God has created a program that is designed to save your planet and he's going to need the animals and children to help him do it."

Bonnie looks confused, "Soooo You and I are going to save the world?"

"Well not just you and I. God has children and animals all over the world working together. We are just one part of it, but an important part, in getting this planet back on track."

"What are we going to do?" asks Bonnie.

"We are going to use this trash that is being dumped in

the ocean and make bricks that will help the rain forests and farmers all over the world."

Bonnie looks at the trash that the pelican has dumped in her sandbox and then looks up to the pelican.

"I don't know how to make bricks from that."

"Well that's why God called me Polly the Professor. Once I show you how to make the bricks, you are going to get other children involved and pretty soon there is going to be all kinds of children in San Diego making bricks and building things. Then your dad, who is a brilliant engineer, is going to help the children take this project to a massive level. We are not only going to clean up the oceans from all the trash, but we are going to save the rain forests and provide farmers all over the world with a real solution to the food problems facing the planet. Wouldn't you like to be a part of that, Bonnie?"

Bonnie raises her eyebrows, "Wow that sounds awesome. When do we start?"

Polly the Professor looks down at the trash she has dumped in the sandbox, "Well Bonnie, if my calculations are correct, I do believe we have enough trash here for one brick." Polly looks at Bonnie, "You want to make a brick now?"

"Sure. What do I need to do?"

"Well I need to go get some kelp – it's part of our secret formula – while you get a bucket to mix stuff, a baking pan that your mother would use for making bread – do you have something like that?"

"I think so."

"Good. Get that … and a pair of good gloves if you have them. This stuff could be nasty, so we want to be sure and wear gloves at all times, okay?"

"Okay. I think I have some gloves that will work." says Bonnie, whose excitement seems to be growing with every word.

"Great. Let's get started. You go get your items and I'll go get my kelp."

"Okay, Polly. Hurry back." she waves to Polly who is heading out to the ocean.

~~~~~~~~~~

"Okay, so we all have our assignments, right?" says Bob as the rest of the animals, Eduardo and Francisco all agree.

"So we have the animals who are going to stop the destruction of the rain forest, but to begin with, we just have to get in the way, alright? Before we can put the animal plan to full execution, we first have to get Eduardo, Francisco and Bird working with the children in California and their brick program. We have a network of animals who will be giving us constant updates from all over the world because it's really important that the animals of the rain forest do not make any major move until we have a solution well on its way to being realized. I need you all to be clear that we do not want to harm anyone or create any environment of disharmony with the earthlings. God doesn't want to just solve the problems, he wants us to do so in a manner that also shows that earthlings and animals can live in harmony. Are there any questions?"

"Yes Bobby, I have a question." says Spider

"Okay." says Bob.

"So God gave us the ability to talk and listen to all the earthlings right? But we can only talk and be heard and understood by the children, right?"

"That is correct." Bob agrees.

"So if I can get a bunch of my brothers to surround a field that is being worked by the earthlings, we can heckle and laugh and throw things at them all we want and they won't understand us, right?"

"Well if you throw things at them, make sure you don't hit them." says Bob

"Oh we don't want to hurt them, we just want to spook 'em a little."

The other animals laugh and give each other high fives, except Snake who just laughs, of course.

"That's fine. But remember that any children working the field will be able to hear and understand you, which is not necessarily a bad thing, but something to be aware of."

"So what age is considered a child?" asks Jaggie

"Up to teenager. Teenagers traditionally don't listen anyway and after teenagers, they become adults and, well, they are the ones who are screwing up everything in the first place. God will only use adults on a very limited basis, like Francisco here, but God would prefer to leave this program to the animals and children under teenager years of age."

"Oh this is going to be so much fun. We are going to be messing with these people every day until the brick program gets up and running." says Spider jumping up and down in enthusiasm.

"Oh if you want to just spook 'em, I can get a bunch or us howlers to sneak up on the field workers and howl pretty loud, ya know. Those people will be wetting their pants in a state of paranoia in a couple of weeks." says Howler as the others drop and roll around in laughter.

"Okay, okay." says Bob as he tries to get their attention again, "Scaring them is fine. If we can get some to quit their jobs because the animals are spooking them, great. But we must remember that we do not want to create enemies. Have fun with it, but always back off before you make them angry. Once the brick program gets fully operational, the rain forests will become your home again and that's what we are all shooting for."

"Well this messing with the earthlings sounds like fun to me. I'm guessing I can get my group to help out with that as well. You tell those kiddos in the brick program to take their time and get it right. I think all of us in the Rain Forest can have a lot of fun in the mean time, right?" says Jaggie to the other animals.

"Okay, then. We all know what needs to be done. We need to break this meeting up so Francisco and Eduardo can get home and Bird can start heading for California." says Bob conclusively.

"Okay Bob!" says the animals in unison as they burst into laughter and head back into the forest.

~~~~~~~~~~

"Wow, that's really cool." says Bonnie as she studies her first brick.

"See how easy that is," says Polly the Professor, "we can use pretty much anything from the trash we collect. The straws make a perfect rebar because the binder solution can get inside as well as around the straw to make it solid. We can also use the straws as connecters to other bricks so they become like legos which will make for a stronger walls. It's light, it's solid, it's durable and there's nothing that is going to hurt the environment."

"That's going to save the planet!" says Bonnie with great enthusiasm. But Polly is quick to cool her off.

"Hold on, honey. That's just one mouth full of trash. There's a lot of trash out there. Before we save the planet, we have a lot more steps to work out."

Bonnie looks at Polly, then at her brick, "So what's the next step?"

"We need to get your dad involved. We can't keep using mom's baking pans, so we need dad to create a mold for making the bricks. So go inside and get paper, a ruler and pencils or crayons, something to write with. You can show him how he can create molds that work with our bricks to build walls that are solid, light and gets rid of the trash that is being dumped into the ocean. You can recruit other children to help you build walls and I can recruit lots of pelicans to bring you the trash. Once your dad sees all the children in his back yard building walls with trash bricks, he'll see opportunity. Once an adult sees opportunity, you just step aside and let them go. Before you know it, there's a big factory taking the trash and making Bonnie Bricks that can be used for any number of construction projects."

"That'd be so cool. I'll go get the stuff to write on." says an enthusiastic Bonnie.

~~~~~~~~~~

God shows up again at the control room of the CARPE DIEM Command Center and asks the angel at the control panel to contact Bird before he leaves for California.

Bird, please come to the control room at CARPE DIEM command center before you head to California.

"Did somebody call me?" says Bird the guardian angel as he makes his way into the control room.

"Yes, come in." says God as he offers Bird a seat.

"Before you head to California, I wanted you to be clear on the brick project going on there." says God.

"Okay" says Bird as he takes his seat next to God.

"You're going to need to hook up with Polly the Professor, a pelican in San Diego who is also the guardian angel of Bonnie."

"Bonnie's guardian angel is named Polly the Professor?" asks Bird.

"Yes …. Do you like it?" asks God.

Bird looks painfully at God, "They named me Bird?"

"Yes, I know. We changed the policy so that guardian angels will now have names before they take assignments at Earth Operations. The CARPE DIEM Plan has certainly showed me that letting others do so can be a bit awkward.

Once your current assignment is completed, we'll get you another name, but for now, we'll just go with Bird."

"Thank you. But you can keep Bob as Bob. Snake was right when he said Bob bobs a lot when he's nervous."

God laughs, "I know. I thought he'd get dizzy and fall off that stump a couple of times when the animals were having fun. He's definitely a Bob."

They both laugh.

"So far, we have a Spot, Peter the female Parrot, Marvin, Bob, Snake, Spider, Howler, Jaggie and Bird…" God shakes his head, "I created a new angel name calling position with a special creative gene that can provide a proper name to every guardian angel coming into Earth Operations from now on. And I have added that under no circumstances will a guardian angel ever be responsible for naming animals or any living things while on assignment."

"Good call, sir" says Bird.

"So, back to Polly the Professor. You'll have to hook up with her when you get to San Diego. She's getting a lot of the pelicans involved with the brick project, so just get to the coast and find any pelican and they will likely know where to find her. Polly has developed a great plan for the brick program which Bonnie is getting a lot of children involved with, so I want you to work with her and make sure the bricks they are making will hold up in the Rain Forest environment. We have to make sure that the solutions we have are going to work. We all know that the adults will always find a reason to reject the solutions which is why the planet is in it's current dismal state. So you work with Polly and oversee the brick program and report back to the center here so we can get Francisco and Eduardo involved on their end. Got it?"

"Yes sir, I got it." says Bird as God stands to leave.

"Well, keep up the good work everyone. Let me know if you need me for anything else." God says as he exits.

~~~~~~~~~~

Bird is perched on the pier in Pacific Beach, exhausted from his long flight. A pelican lands next to him.

"You look a bit out of sorts little fella. You new to the area?"

"Yes. I just flew up from the rain forests of Brazil."

"Welcome to San Diego, mate. What brings you to our fine slice of paradise?"

"I'm looking for a pelican named Polly the Professor. Do you know where I can find her?"

"Everyone knows the professor here. She has us all collecting trash from the ocean and bringing it to this girl she's working with."

"Bonnie?"

"Yea, that's her name. Do you know Bonnie?"

"No, I was sent up here to help out with the brick program." says Bird, still out of breath.

The pelican looks Bird over, "Well you're a bit short and I'm not sure that beak of yours is going to hold much trash, so I'm not sure how much help you'll be."

"I'm not here to collect trash, I'm here to work with

Bonnie and Polly to make sure the bricks work well for our rain forest project."

"So you just need to get to Bonnie's place then. I just came from there – heading out for another load now. She lives about ten blocks up due east. Stay even with this pier and head east and you can't miss it. A blue house with a back yard full of kids making bricks. If you got here from Brazil, I'm sure you can find Bonnie's place. Good luck, pal. I gotta head out."

With that, the pelican flies out to sea while Bird looks back towards land.

"Okay, ten more blocks and I'm done." says Bird as he lifts off and catches the breeze coming off the ocean and calmly heads east.

There it is, thinks Bird as he looks down on a back yard full of kids and pelicans busily building bricks. Easy to find this place, as he flies down to take a rest on the fence.

"Excuse me young man, excuse me." calls out Bird to a young boy standing just below.

The boy turns his head upward, "You talking to me?"

"Yes, I'm looking for a Bonnie. Could you point her out to me?"

"Bonnie!" screams the boy and startles Bird. Bonnie comes over, "This little bird is looking for you."

Bonnie looks up at Bird and gives him the once over with an expression that is not impressed. "Can I help you?"

"Yes, my name is," he pauses and clears his throat, "Bird

and I just flew up from Brazil to work with a pelican named Polly the Professor, she's your guardian angel, I understand?"

"She is. You want to talk to her?" says Bonnie.

"I would like that very much." says Bird

"Hey, Professor. This is Bird and he just flew up here from Brazil to talk to you." she says to the pelican perched on the fence a few feet to Birds left.

Polly looks over to Bird and moves a couple steps over, "I'm Polly, what can I do for you?"

"Yes, I'm from Brazil,…"

Polly interrupts, "Wait, you're name is Bird?"

"Yes." says Bird with a dose of embarrassment.

"You're the guardian angel for … what's his name …. oh, Francisco, right?"

"Yes, Francisco."

"I've heard about you. You're the reason I got my name. When they named you Bird, God changed the policy and now he's naming the guardian angels before they go on assignment."

"Yes, I am aware of that. God told me he created a new angel in charge of giving angels names before they work at Earth Operations."

"Good move, right?"

"Yes. He assured me that I could get a new name after this assignment is over."

"I'm sure you'll appreciate that. So what can I do for you, Bird?" says Polly with smile trying to keep in a laughter.

"Well, like I was saying, I flew up here from Brazil, because…"

"Wait a minute it. You flew all the way here from Brazil?" Polly asks.

"Well that's where I came from. The rain forests in Brazil." says Bird a bit miffed at the questioning.

"How come you didn't just come directly from the CARPE DIEM command center? That's a 5,000 mile trip flying. You coulda been here months ago if you just came directly from the command center." Polly says with an overload of curiosity.

Bird just stares at Polly for an uncomfortable amount of time before Polly breaks the silence.

"You didn't know you could do that?" Polly asks in an almost whisper.

Bird just stares at Polly.

"Okay, then. Well I'm sure it was a scenic flight and you look to be in great shape, so let's move on shall we." says Polly, desperately trying not to laugh while Bird is being smothered with humility.

"As you can see, Bird, we have made some good progress while you've been flying, and things are progressing well. Bonnie's dad has really been a great help. He's got a patent on his brick making system and is looking for a big warehouse in the area where he can get the children involved making bricks.

"I think that's what God wanted you to come up here for. We need a big order of bricks in order to have the resources to really bring it all to the next level. We have some non-profits helping the pelicans get the trash and we need to have a warehouse to put all the trash in and build a bigger scale brick maker because Bonnie's mom wants her back yard back, you can understand that, right?"

Polly takes a breath to give Bird, who is staring out, unable to focus beyond the humility, a chance to speak, which Polly quickly sees is not going to happen, so she continues.

"Anyway, things are going great here, so we just need you to go back to Francisco to get his government to make an order for these bricks so we can have the resources to put it all together. Bonnie's dad assures us that the bricks will be perfect for the rain forest environment, so you just have to get that order in, okay?" Polly pauses and leans over towards Bird, "And in the interest of time, I'd prefer you go back to Brazil via the Command Center this time, if that's okay."

"Of course," says Bird in a very unemotional tone, "I'll make sure Francisco gets that order in right away. Just have Bonnie send me the contact information to my number at the command center and I'll make sure Francisco gives her dad a formal call."

With that, Bird flies off as Bonnie looks at Polly, "He flew all the way from Brazil?"

Polly, unable to hold it any longer, falls off the fence and rolls in the sandbox laughing uncontrollably.

Meanwhile, Bird finds himself sitting in his cubical at the command center when a guardian angel blurts out, "Hey Bird, Ya want to fly to the North Pole when this is all over?"

As the room of angels explodes into laughter as Bird stares at the contact information for Bonnie's dad staring back at him. An angel sitting next to him leans over and quietly clicks on the blue 'destination' button on the bottom of Birds screen and says, "You just type in your destination and when you leave, you're there." the angel looks at Bird, who looks at him and says "I see."

The CARPE DIEM Command Center is out of control with laughter.

~~~~~~~~~~

God makes his way into the control booth at CARPE DIEM command center and takes a seat.

"So how are things going with the CARPE DIEM Plan?"

"Well sir, the poaching issue continues to be a thing of the past...."

"A dead issue, right?" God says with a smile.

"Yes sir. And the Brick program had some delays, but everything has worked out and it looks to be moving forward nicely as well."

"What kind of delays?" asks God.

"Well sir, it appears that Bird thought you wanted him to be a migratory bird because you wanted him to fly to San Diego."

"Excuse me? Are you saying Bird flew from Brazil to San Diego? That's over 5000 miles." says God baffled.

"Yes sir"

"Did he not know about the blue button on his monitor?"

"Apparently not sir."

"How long did it take him?"

"A little over two months sir."

"We lost two months because he thought I wanted him to fly from Brazil to San Diego? I wanted him to be a migratory bird because it would make more sense when he went to San Diego instead of being a Toucan. Your saying he didn't realize that?"

"Apparently not sir."

God takes a moment to let this sink in.

"How's he doing now?" asks God.

"Well sir, he's working well with Francisco and Eduardo, so things are going well in the rain forests. The other angels here at the command center have been pretty brutal on him though. Do you want me to have them back off?"

"They're all doing their jobs, right?"

"Yes sir."

"Then let them have their fun with it. I don't want to hear any more issues with the blue buttons."

"That should not be an issue any more sir."

"Great, so let's get back to the actual issues of planet earth. How's the brick program going?"

"Excellent, sir. Bonnie's dad quit his corporate job and has developed a lot of equipment that is making it hard for the farmers to say no to. His company has gone public and is making a lot of money to finance the program, so we are seeing more and more farmers developing their crops by using 500 acres of stacked crops on 25 acres. And the side product is that they are also planting a lot of trees on the remaining acres to help build the natural ecosystem in many of the areas. We are starting to see some real results so far and the general public has really embraced the technology."

"That's great!. So I'm guessing we just have to let it take it's course then?'

"Yes sir. There have been some added side benefits from smart people who are now paying attention, who are developing other products and systems to help the environment which is normal for these kind of situations."

"No doubt. Once one person starts making a boat load of money, the smart people start getting involved. That's okay as long as it's protecting the planet and the children are getting the credit. Speaking of, how's Bonnie doing?"

"She's doing good. She's been working with her dad of course and she'll be heading off to college in a few weeks."

"Excuse me? I thought she was eight?"

"Remember sir, we don't have time on this side. The good news is that many of the children that we got involved with the animals when we started CARPE DIEM are now in high school or going to college. They are already calling them the CARPE DIEM generation."

"Wow. Starting college already. I know I created it that way, but sometimes trying to work on this side with the earthlings on that side sure gets me confused."

"How's the other issues doing?" he asks.

"Good. The pollution in China and India has really turned around. It's like you always say, sir. Once you get their attention, everyone wants to jump on board. It seems China and India were feeling left out of the environmental conversation, so they quickly challenged their rank and file to focus on cleaning the air and water. Their commitment has been impressive too. Looks like everyone is getting into the act sir."

God stands, "That sounds great fellas. Keep me informed. And do not let any angel go without a reminder of the blue button. We wasted two months for crying out loud."

"Excuse me, God. There is a Charles Sodah in DOG central requesting a meeting with you." says an angel who has come through the door.

"Well, gotta go fellas. Keep up the nice work."

11

Furat and the DOG

"So that's the deal then?" asks God.

"Yes. I was well aware of Amaan when I was on the other side. He has lots of money, lots of power and though he has a presence on the world stage as a decent, compassionate man, his underworld network that he controls is ruthless. Many who have power and money like Amaan understand that he will not hesitate to eliminate anyone who gets in the way of his agenda. I'm afraid Furat is unaware that her dad is an undercover soldier for Amaan. She could be putting her family in grave danger if she continues with her work." says Charles.

"I see." says God as he considers the information Charles has brought him, as an angel opens the door to the room they are meeting in.

"Yes sir." says the angel.

"Get me Abdul Raheem please."

As the angel leaves, God looks to Charles. "So your work here at DOG central is going well?"

Charles hesitates, "Well I'm not sure how much help I'm providing. Sometimes I feel like I'm learning more from the kids than they are learning from me."

God smiles, "Yes, the children have a keen sense of fairness and common sense that adults like yourself tend to lose when they focus on wealth and power. I have no doubt, Mr. Sodah, that you will learn much more from listening to the children, than they will listening to you."

At that, the door opens and Abdul Raheem comes in.

"Do you need me sir?" says Raheem who stands in a very respectful manner.

"Ah yes, Abdul, come in. I suppose you know Mr. Sodah?"

"I am aware of Mr. Sodah, sir. Very wealthy man."

"Well he's not very wealthy on this side." says God.

"The only currency on this side is Love, sir." says Abdul.

God looks to Charles who looks as if he is seeing a ghost. "I take it you know Abdul Raheem, Charles?"

Charles looks at God with fear, "He's the terrorist who ruthlessly killed so many innocent people." says Charles in a confused tone.

"That is true, Mr. Sodah. There were many lives ruined because of the two of you. The difference is that Abdul was fortunate enough to get a hug from a little girl that softened his heart shortly before he crossed over to this side, isn't that right Abdul?"

"Oh, yes sir. I will forever be grateful for Little One's hug." says Abdul.

God looks to Charles, "He's one of my best ambassadors of Love, Charles. Maybe you can learn something from him." God smiles as he offers Abdul a seat.

"I called you here, Abdul, because I think you could be of great service to a situation Charles has brought to my attention."

"Yes sir. I'd be happy to be of service." says Abdul.

God pulls up a picture of Amaan on the wall of the room, "Are you familiar with this man Abdul?"

"Yes sir. Very rich man. Very dangerous man."

God pulls up a picture of a little girl.

"This girl is named Furat. She is very active little girl in her school's environmental program. A very good girl who is absolutely dedicated to saving the planet. Smart, too. Very good at science and hopes to grow up to be a science engineer and develop new technologies that will move the world away from dependency on oil and other pollutant chemicals."

"Very good girl, indeed sir." says Abdul.

"Yes, but she was talking to Charles here about her frustration in being unable to get her father's support. Her father, Saeed is a smart man who works at a big refinery owned by Amaan. Furat is unaware that Saeed is a high ranking soldier in Amaan's underground activities. Furat doesn't understand that her father's lack of encouragement with her environmental activities is a lot more than just being an unsupportive father, but in reality, her efforts are putting her family, and her father specifically, in grave danger."

"Oh yes sir. Amaan would not hesitate to get rid of that family for sure." says Abdul.

"That's why I called you in, Abdul. I need you to be involved with Furat and her family. It's a delicate situation that will require someone like you, who is familiar with how the mind of a terrorist like Amaan works and help Furat achieve her environmental goals without endangering her family. It won't be easy, but if we do it right, this could be a huge win for planet Earth." says God.

"It would be an honor to help, sir. What can I do?"

"I want you to become a stray dog in Furat's world. You will have the ability to talk with her and I will have her guardian angel visit her right away to explain the plan to her. At no time do I want Furat to hear about her father's secret life as a soldier for Amaan. We don't want to break hearts, we want to win hearts over for love."

"Yes sir. I will not let you down." says Abdul, "When do you want me to start?"

"Well she walks to school every day, so it will be easy for you to be a stray dog who happens to befriend her on her way to school. I'll have her guardian angel talk to her tonight, so she is not alarmed when you – a dog – starts talking to her. I will be available at any moment for any situations that might come up. This could become a tragedy quickly, so it's important that we all stay on top of this until it's resolved."

"I will be a great friend to Furat and protect her. We

will get the results needed to promote love." says an excited Abdul.

"I know you do not like thinking about your past, Abdul, but I need you on this one to go back to your days as a terrorist and think like Amaan so you can better steer Furat without endangering her family."

"I will use my past to serve the future of love, sir."

"Well that should do it fellas. Any questions?" says God.

Charles speaks up for the first time, "What do you want me to do?"

"You will have an open line to Abdul at all times. Abdul has the mind of a terrorist, but you have the mind of the wealthy greed. You need to monitor Amaan at all times and let Abdul know of any changes in his behavior or conversation that might endanger others. Every time Furat is in school or at home, I want the two of you to be talking and planning the next step. It is vital that the two of you work together on this, got it?"

"Yes sir, we will not let you down." says Abdul as Charles just sits there still a bit uncertain.

God notices, "You can go back to your cubical and observe Amaan on your monitor. You will not take any more calls until after this situation is resolved. I want you to observe Amaan and let Abdul know anything that will help him with his work with Furat. Do you understand?"

"Yes."

As God gets up to leave, he turns to Charles, "And thank

you for bringing this to my attention. There just might be some hope for your heart after all, right?" he smiles.

For the first time since he came to the other side, Charles cracks a subtle smile as God leaves, Abdul leaves to become Furats best friend and Charles gets up to head back to his cubical.

~~~~~~~~~~

"Furat, Furat, Wake up." says the guardian angel who has taken over Furats stuffed turtle on her bed. "Psssst, Furat, wake up."

Furat sits up, shakes her head and looks around for whoever it is trying to wake her up, then looks down at her favorite stuffed animal.

"Furat, I'm your guardian angel. I have to take on a physical presence in order to talk to you, so I took over Leo, your stuffed turtle. Nobody can hear me but you, so talk softly or your parents will think you are crazy, got it?"

Furat stares at the turtle a bit uncertain.

"You're my guardian angel?" she asks the turtle.

"Yes, and I need to talk to you about a plan God has that he needs your help with."

"God needs my help? I'm just a kid." says Furat, a bit surprised.

"Trust me, Furat. God would rather work with kids over adults any time he can. Adults are the ones who create the problems for the most part."

Furat thinks about it and agrees, "They sure are messing up the planet, that's for sure."

"Exactly. And God really likes how you are working with your environmental group at school and the effort you are making to stop the pollution."

"Well it's not very easy to get people to understand." says the girl, a bit perplexed.

"Yes, we know. That's why God wants to help you. But first you must understand that a lot of people around here work at the refinery like your dad. You must be careful with what you are doing because your dad could lose his job. His job provides the home you live in, the food you have to eat and the clothes you wear to school. That's why God wants to give you a helper."

"God's giving me a helper?"

"Yes. On your way to school tomorrow, you will have a stray dog that will serve as your helper. God gave the dog the ability to talk with you, so it's really important that you listen to this dog. Remember that only you can hear the dog so you need to remember to step away where no one can see you talking, okay?"

"The dog is going to help me with the environment? Is he a guardian angel, too?"

"No, he's not an angel, just a special assignment ambassador who knows a lot about the situation who can help you a lot, so it's important that you listen carefully to everything he says, okay?"

"Does this dog have a name?" she asks out of curiosity.

"No. You are welcome to give him a name if it makes it easier for you, but do not call him Spot."

"Spot? Why would anyone call their dog Spot? Does he have a lot of spots?" asks Furat, a bit baffled by the request.

"No. No spots. He's a mutt. God would just prefer you call him something else, okay?"

"Okay. Maybe I'll call him Squares." she says with a giggle as Leo rolls her eyes.

""Just be creative and don't spend a lot of time thinking of a name. This dog will be a great help to you under very sensitive circumstances. It's really important to remember that what you and your class mates are doing is really good and important to the world, but it also goes against what your dad and many of the other parents in your school are doing at the refinery. You must be careful. That's why God is giving you a helper, so pay attention to your stray dog."

"Okay. I'll be careful. Are you going to be in Leo from now on?"

"No. Only when I need to talk with you. But our hearts are always connected, and the wristband on your arm can let you contact me at any time. The pink button contacts me, the green button will get you the stray dog, and the brown DOG button I can explain to you later, but you'll not need it because the stray dog you are working with will be using that one. So if I sense anything that requires my help, just push the pink button and I'll be able to help you out, got it?"

"Got it."

"Okay then. Lay back down and get some rest. You're going to do some wonderful things and God really appreciates what you are doing."

Furat lays down as Leo the guardian angel turtle heads back to CARPE DIEM central.

~~~~~~~~~~

"Furat?" says Abdul the stray dog as Furat approaches on her way to school.

"Are you my stray dog helper that God sent." says Furat with excitement as she runs up to the dog.

"Quiet now, please follow me. We don't want others to see you talking to a dog."

"It's okay. I stop and talk to dogs all the time. There's nothing wrong with that." says Furat with a relaxed tone.

"Well yes I suppose children do that a lot, but I need to talk with you and would prefer we do so unnoticed." says Abdul the dog as he leads her back to a thicket of bushes.

"This is good. We'll meet here every day until we have the results God is looking for if that is okay with you."

"Sure. Do you have a name? Leo, my guardian angel turtle said I could give you name, as long as it's not Spot."

"Spot? Why would anyone call their dog Spot? Just call me Raheem, okay?"

Furat thinks about it, then shrugs her shoulders, "I guess Raheem is better than Spot."

"Good girl. Now today I just wanted to make contact with you and let you know that I will be here every day before and after school to help you with your environmental work, so you might want to leave every morning a few minutes earlier. I don't want you to be late for school."

"Okay Raheem. So what do you want me to do today?"

"Nothing yet. What you are doing is really, really good and God is very proud of you. But we have to be very careful because so many of the parents work at the refinery like your dad, so we have to think about every move we make so we don't get your parents fired from their job, okay?"

"Okay. I promise to tell you what we are planning, but we won't do anything unless you say it's okay, okay?"

"Perfect. You are a good girl Furat. I'm looking forward to working with you and the other children."

"Can I bring some of the other kids here after school?"

"Not yet, Furat. We want to be safe. We can not draw any suspicion to our meetings or endanger any of the children unnecessarily. Your dad is a very good man with a good heart, Furat, but the man who owns the refinery is a very bad man who would do anything to protect his wealth. We must be careful, little one."

"Okay, Raheem. I'll let the others know that we should be careful."

"Good girl. Now off to school with you. The more you learn, the more your love grows, little one."

"See you after school Raheem." says Furat as she skips off to school and Raheem heads towards the refinery to snoop around.

~~~~~~~~~~

"How's the wonderful world of CARPE DIEM?" says God as he bounces into the control booth at CARPE DIEM command center of Earth Operations and takes a seat.

"Going well, sir. Most areas of concern are making nice

progress. The children and animals are really doing a great job."

"Excellent! I always say that any program that doesn't involve adult earthlings is going to succeed. What good news do you have for me?"

"Well there was a major breakthrough with the Coltan mineral issue."

"Oh yes, refresh my memory now, what was the issue there?"

"They use a lot of the Coltan in mobile phones, computers and high-tech toys. The mineral is mostly found in the Congo of Central Africa. With all the mining of Coltan in the Congo, the Gorillas have become dangerously endangered because so much of their habitat is being mined for Coltan."

"Ahhh yes. I swear I gave the earthlings the brains to figure this stuff out. I put a lot of minerals in the earth that is beneficial to the various cycles of life and needs to stay in the earth. They have the capacity to take one small sample of any mineral and with their intelligence create a synthetic copy of every mineral that they could use for all their progress without any harm to the earth itself. You'd think they would have figured that out by now. But I guess it's easier for them to just destroy the earth by digging up the stuff. And they say they are at the top of the food chain. Idiots." God says shaking his head.

"Yes, well that's the good news sir. It seems a young boy in the Congo who was working with the Gorillas contacted a young girl whose father is a scientist in Silicon Valley and practically gave her the recipe for this synthetic material that would be more effective with the high tech manufacturing. Her father tried it and it worked great. Now this scientist is making millions and the children and gorillas in the Congo are blocking the roads into the mining camps. Look at this report that was just aired."

God looks over to the monitor.

In environmental news, there are reports from the Congo of children and gorillas blocking the roads into mining camps. You heard that right. It appears that the gorillas and children are somehow working side by side to block all the workers from getting into the mining camps that are destroying the gorillas habitat. We sent our own Richard Stevens to investigate.

Thanks, Judy.

I am standing here at one of the roads that leads to a mining camp about a mile down the road. As you can see, the children and gorillas have been keeping a vigil round the clock to keep this road – and other roads leading into other mines blocked. I spoke with a spokesperson for the children.

First, let me ask you how it is that these children are able to work side by side with these dangerous animals like they do?

Well they are only dangerous when they feel threatened and all these children come from villages near their habitats and are very comfortable working with the gorillas.

So what is the message they are trying to present?

The miners have been mining Coltan for years which is used in computers and phones throughout the world. Scientists have created a new synthetic material that can be used instead of Coltan which is more effective and can be mass produced in laboratories all over the world. The gorillas are an endangered species because the mining has made their habitat become uninhabitable, but with a new product being developed on a massive scale, the children and gorillas are forcing the issue that the Congo is no longer open for business.

Judy, I checked this out and found out that there is a new synthetic material developed in Silicon Valley that everyone says will be much better material for the high-tech industry without doing any further harm to the environment. It looks like the children have got this right, Judy.

And on a side note, I can report that while the children and gorillas have been blocking the miners from going in, there has been a network of environmentalists that have been secretly sneaking into the mine areas and planting trees all around in hopes of restoring the gorillas habitat.

So it looks like the mining industry in the Congo is a thing of the past.

Back to you Judy.

God stands up clapping. "I knew it. Leave it to the kids and animals to figure this stuff out. Now we didn't actually give the children the recipe for the synthetic material, did we? I didn't want us to be just throwing the recipes at the earthlings, remember."

"Well not really sir. The guardian angel for the boy went

out of his way to sound vague, saying if you possibly took one chemical, say this one and put it with another chemical, say that one and possibly made the properties conducive to electrical current, there would be potentially the ability of creating a material that could eliminate the need for any more Coltan? I think the boy understood enough and went with it. Was that cheating, sir?"

God smiles, "Close, but those earthlings love to speak hypothetically anyway, so I'm sure the angel was just trying to speak their language, right? Besides, I love the gorillas and we are running out of time. I'll take it as is."

God gets up to leave before asking, "How's the situation with Abdul and Furat going?"

"Good. Raheem has been very careful to help Furat keep a low profile with her environmental work and Mr. Sodah has been able to send many mixed messages to Amaan that has created a great deal of in house bickering. It's in a critical stage now as Amaan is getting frustrated so Charles and Abdul are working hard to keep things from exploding out of control while encouraging the children to keep working with their concerns. We are cautiously optimistic."

God shakes his head, "If we can win that battle, we can all be optimistic. Keep me posted." as he leaves the control booth.

~~~~~~~~~~

"Sir, there is a Saeed Iman here to see you." says the man at the door to the office of Amaan.

"Yes, send him in."

Saeed is Furat's father who loves his daughter very much and has been conflicted between her passion for the environment and his work at Amaan's refinery.

"Thank you, sir, for giving me this time. I know you are busy." says Saeed.

"I was told that you have a proposal that I need to hear about?"

"Yes sir."

"Please sit down. When they told me you had a plan, I had my assistants bring me your records. You've been a very loyal worker for me for many years."

"Yes sir. I very much appreciate the opportunity to work at the refinery."

"I also understand that you have a daughter who is very active in her school with an environmental club?"

"Yes sir." says Saeed who is becoming quite nervous.

"Is your daughter aware that the clothes she wears, the food she eats and the roof over her head comes from me, and that she would lose it all if you were to go home today without a job at the refinery?"

"Yes sir, she is aware."

"Are you unable to control your daughter's behavior, Mr. Iman?"

"No sir. She is a good girl, sir."

"I would suggest otherwise. I certainly hope that this plan that they are talking about has something to do with correcting your daughter's behavior because it would be a most unfortunate world for a girl to grow up in a fatherless home, wouldn't you agree?"

"Most unfortunate, yes sir."

Amaan glares at Saeed who is squirming in his chair desperately trying not to let fear overwhelm him.

"I let you have this meeting with me because some of my most trusted advisors said your plan is well worth looking into. I certainly hope so, Mr. Iman, because if this plan does not excite me, your future will have no plans. Do you understand what I am saying?"

"Yes sir."

After a very uncomfortable pause, Amaan continues.

"I am a very busy man Mr. Iman. Your plan?"

"Yes sir. I was with my daughter at the science fair in her school and I happen to see a display from a young boy that truly intrigued me...."

~~~~~~~~~~

God rushes into the CARPE DIEM control booth.

"I came as soon as I could." he pauses as he looks out over the room full of guardian angels. There is an eerie silence as all the angels are sitting back in their desks watching the big monitor with absolute intensity.

"What's going on?" God asks the angel at the control panel.

"The man speaking is Furat's father. He is selling a plan to Amaan that could make Amaan a very, very wealthy man. But if Amaan doesn't take it, it could make Furat a fatherless girl."

"Where did the plan come from?" asks God.

"It actually came from Mr. Sodah at the DOG central. He gave the information to the guardian angel of a boy who is a friend of Furats and his father is a science professor at the university. Saeed – Furat's father- saw the experiment at the school's science fair and tried it out and it worked beautifully, so now he's trying to get Amaan to see the benefits of developing this new technology. It's a very critical time."

"Get me Charles Sodah immediately." God instructs the angel at the door.

Charles comes into the booth, "You wish to see me sir?"

"Yes, sit down." God says as he moves over one seat and offers Charles the other.

"Tell me about this plan Saeed is selling. Where did you get it?"

Charles hesitates, but knows he has to come clean.

"A man gave me the plan when I was on the other side. It was a brilliant plan, but I wasn't one to take risks at the time, so I buried it to make sure no one else got it."

"And what became of the man who created it?"

Charles hesitates and bows his head.

"I paid him a million dollars a year as long as he kept quiet about the plan."

"And how many years did that add up to?"

Charles slumps even further into his seat.

"He died in a boat accident three months later."

"And tell me, Charles, was this truly an accident?"

"No sir. I was not a man who took risks. I couldn't afford to have him say anything about his plan, so I had him removed."

"I appreciate your honesty, Charles. His name was Mark Fredricks. His wife, Susan, was on that boat too. They had three children who were left without parents because of you. The good news is that your last will was pathetic. You had all that money and you only left it to a couple of non-profits that were as crooked as you. Fortunately, I was able to add a few items on your last will and you'll be happy to know that those three children will get one million dollars a year for life. And I even added a stipulation that each of their children would also get the payout continuously for five consecutive generations before those crooked non-profits can have a dime."

God pauses to let this sink in for Charles.

"You know Charles, a man with so much money as you had should have a last will that reflects some generosity, don't you think?"

Charles quietly, without looking up, says "Yes sir."

"You may go back to the DOG House, Mr. Sodah. But let me say before you leave that I truly appreciate you giving this information to the guardian angel of this boy. I continue to feel optimistic about your heart and your work here, Charles. If this has a positive outcome, I want you to appreciate your participation in a very positive outcome for love."

"Yes sir." says Charles as he gets up to leave.

~~~~~~~~~~

"Do you know this boy who made the exhibit?" asks Amaad.

"Yes sir. He is a very smart boy who is in the environmental club with my daughter." responds Saeed.

"And his father?"

"His father is a Science professor at the local university. He helped his son problem solve his experiment. Very smart man."

"And how do you want me to respond when this man tells everyone that I stole his sons idea in order to keep everyone else from looking at me like the scum of the earth?"

"You tell them the truth, sir."

"Excuse me?" says Amaan with a strong tone of disbelief.

"Well sir, you tell everyone that you got the idea from one of your lab workers who saw it at a school science fair. He checked it out and it worked perfectly, so you decided to get behind the idea. You give the school enough money to make them happy. You offer the boys father a salary that will make the university salary look like lunch money to run your new research and development facility and everyone looks at you as a hero while you make even more money because you'll be on both sides of the issue. You'll still have the refinery to provide those many other uses of oil in the world, while at the same time be leading the way on a new technology that will reinvent the way we travel in an environmentally friendly way. Everyone is happy, as your wealth increases many fold."

Amaan sits back in his overstuffed office chair to consider everything. After what seemed like an eternity, he reaches over and pushes a button.

"Tell Asaad to come in here at once." he says.

Amaan remains quiet as Saeed sits nervously.

"Did you call me sir?" says Asaad as he walks into the office.

"You are the one who told me I should listen to this plan?"

"Yes sir."

"And you recommend that I move forward with it even though you understand that if it fails, you fail as well?"

Asaad looks at Amaan, fully aware of what he is saying.

"Yes sir. I had some of our most intelligent scientists look at it and they all agreed this is a brilliant plan sir."

"Very well. You may leave."

As Asaad walks out, Amaan turns his attention to Saeed, who remains frozen in anticipation.

"Well, Mr. Iman, it appears that your daughter will have a father for the foreseeable future. " He smiles at Saeed who is finally breathing again. "You are a good, loyal worker for me Saeed. If this goes as everyone says it will, I will remember the one who brought me the idea. You have not disappointed me today Saeed. I will not disappoint you or your family. You may go back to work now."

"Thank you sir." says Saeed as he gets up and makes his way to the door as Amaan pushes the button again.

"Schedule a meeting with my top engineers first thing in the morning. We have to build a new factory."

"Yes sir. Right away." as Amaan sits back with a big grin.

~~~~~~~~~~

Back at the CARPE DIEM command center the silent room of angels explodes into cheers as the monitor shows

Saeed falling to one knee outside, overwhelmed by tears of gratitude that his risk paid off.

God stands and leans over to the microphone and with great enthusiasm says, "Now that's how you save planet Earth angels! Nice work everyone!" which escalates the celebration on the floor to out of control, as God pats the back of the angel at the control panel as he makes his way to the door.

Meanwhile, in DOG central, Charles sits back, takes his headset off, covers his face with his hands and weeps.

12

Kashi, Deepak, Madhuri and Hari

Kashi and Deepak are best friends who live in the same village and walk to school together every day. Kashi is a very smart girl who wants to be a scientist when she grows up so she can find answers to the many environmental issues facing her home in India. Deepak loves animals and wants to be a park ranger when he grows up.

Every day as they make their journey from their village to the nearest school, some three miles away, Kashi and Deepak spend the time in wild imagination of how they will fix the many problems facing India today. They are very competitive with each other trying to come up with better solutions than the other. The walk is mostly rural until they get to the outskirts of New Delhi where they go to school.

On this particular morning, as they were about half way to school, they came across a cow with a Rhesus Macaques monkey on it's back. This was not unusual as cows were considered sacred to the people of India and the monkeys seemed to have free reign in India and could be found pretty much wherever they wanted to be.

"What's happening, kiddos?" says the monkey.

Kashi and Deepak stop and look at each other, then at the monkey.

"Ya got a minute?" asks the monkey.

Deepak hesitates, "You're a talking monkey."

"Oh, a brilliant boy at that. My name is Hari, but you can call me Hari. Not only can I talk, but my friend here, Madhuri, can talk as well. Say hello to the kids Madhuri."

The cow looks up to the kids, "How 'ya doin?"

Deepak and Kashi look at each other again before Kashi asks, "How come you can talk?"

"Madhuri and I want to help you out and we can't do much if we can't communicate with you, right?"

"Help us out with what?" says Deepak.

"Save India, of course." says Hari.

"You and the cow are suppose to help me and Deepak save India?" says Kashi.

Hari and Madhuri stare at the kids before Hari continues, "Haven't you heard of the CARPE DIEM Plan?" he asks.

"The Carpe what?" says Deepak with a confused look.

Hari whispers in Madhuri's ear, "You sure we got the right kids Maddie?"

"We were told that all children would be able to talk with us and would know about the CARPE DIEM plan." says Madhuri

Hari stands up straight and stares at the two children, as they stare back.

"Um, we really need to get to school. Can we help you save India some other time?" says Kashi.

Hari has a look of frustration, "Sure kids, you run along to school now. Do your homework and … feed the monkeys." he says.

As Deepak and Kashi head down the trail, Hari and Madhuri walk away grumbling and arguing about what just happened.

~~~~~~~~~~

"Get me Deepak and Kashi's guardian angels!" says God as he storms into the control booth of the CARPE DIEM command center.

Would the guardian angels of Deepak and Kashi report to the control booth please

God grabs the microphone, "NOW!" as all the angels in the command center turn their heads to look at the control booth with much fear.

The two guardian angels enter the control booth.

"Please sit down," says God as he offers them a seat, "And explain to me what exactly are you doing for the CARPE DIEM Plan with your earthlings?" asks God trying desperately to stay calm.

"Well sir, "says Kashi's guardian angel with great enthusiasm, "We figured since these two kids are best of friends and have to walk quite a distance to school every day, that we would feed them ideas to debate about solving the environmental issues on their way to school. Then we keep them focused on their school work, see, so they can get into a really good university when they get older, get an impressive degree in their fields and when they get a job, they'll be well equipped to apply those solutions they debated on their way to school back when they were kids. We are confident, sir, that those two will be heroes of their generation by the time they are forty years old!" says Kashi's angel as both angels sit back in their seats with wide grins of appreciation for their brilliant plan.

God stares at each one back and forth without a word until their enthusiastic grins of appreciation slowly slides into an expression of concern that their brilliant plan is not being embraced.

"Have you looked at India?" asks God.

"Yes sir," responds Deepak's angel, "That's why these debates on the way to school are so…."

God cuts him off, "Those debates are merely words until you put feet on them. India doesn't have any time to waste. India doesn't have time to wait for these kids to grow up. Those kids need to stop talking and start doing. I want you both to visit them tonight and I strongly suggest that you explain to them about the CARPE DIEM Plan – which I will remind you means SIEZE THE MOMENT – that Hari and Madhuri were talking about and tomorrow when Hari and Madhuri talk to them again, I better see a much better reaction from those kids. The CARPE DIEM Plan is for the children and animals to seize the moment NOW, not some day down the road. That's why the earth is in this mess in the first place. You have too many young people getting educated and thinking that they are so intellectual and can figure everything out, then go out into the world as adults and screw everything up. The problem with these adults isn't intellectual, it's that they forget the passions they had as children that is vital to drive their intelligence in a positive direction. We need to tap into the passion of these children right now and with the help of the animals, become the solution that will save the earth NOW, not somewhere down the road."

God stares again back and forth to the two angels who are sitting there completely numb of expression. After a most uncomfortable time of silence, God finishes.

"You need to go talk to your kids with a strong dose of urgency. I better see a better response tomorrow from those kids when Hari and Madhuri talk to them. I assure you both, you do not want me to have to call you into this booth a second time. Do you understand the plan now?"

"Yes sir…. absolutely…. we've got this sir… no problem at all sir.. we are all over this plan, sir." they both say in unison with a frightful tone of overkill.

"You may go." says God as the two angels don't hesitate to bolt out of the control booth.

God sits back in his seat shaking his head but with a smile.

"Do you think they'll get it right this time?" says the angel at the controls.

God smiles, "When I created the guardian angels for earth

operations, I gave them a strong dose of thinking practical and logical so they could be a calming presence for the emotional earthlings. I pretty much figured when I created the CARPE DIEM Plan that there would be angels flying from Brazil to San Diego and angels tripping over the urgency of the moment." God pauses as he gets up to leave and looks out over the many guardian angels busily working his plan, "I'm pretty sure I got many of these angels out of their comfort zone, but they're good angels. They're doing a great job. If I have to pick them up now and then when they trip up, I'm happy to do so." he pats the angel on the back as he moves towards the exit, "Let me know if you need anything."

~~~~~~~~~~

"We're coming up to where we saw them yesterday, right?" says Kashi.

"I think it was right around this bend here." says Deepak.

"There they are!" says Kashi as they both run up to greet Hari and Madhuri.

"We're glad you're here, "says Deepak, "Sorry about yesterday. Our guardian angels had a little misunderstanding about the CARPE DIEM Plan."

"Yeah, but they talked to us last night so now we understand." says Kashi with excitement.

Hari leans down to Madhuri's ear, "I'm sure glad God didn't give us guardian angels, right?"

"Actually, he did. The earthlings are supposed to be our

guardian angels." responds Madhuri with a hint of futile sarcasm as Hari slowly rises with a pained look on his face.

"So," says Hari to the children, "Let's review. The CARPE DIEM Plan has the animals – that's us – working with the children – that's you – together to save the planet. In order for this to work, the animals have the ability to talk and understand the children. Understood?"

"Yes, but there are so many problems where do we even begin?" says Kashi.

Hari points to a plastic bag clinging to a small plant, "There is your starting point."

The two children look at the plastic bag, then back to Hari and Madhuri with expressions of cluelessness as Madhuri explains.

"The key is not to look at all the problems facing India. If we look at the big picture, we'll just tell God to throw the rock and put us out of our misery. We need to take baby steps here."

"Okay, so what's the first baby step?" says Deepak.

"Trash," says Hari, "We need to set an example to the adults that you can't just throw trash on the ground. On your way to school and on the way home, we need you to pick up the trash."

"But what do we do with all this trash?" asks Kashi.

Hari pauses, "Not sure. But God assures us that he has a plan for it, so we'll just trust that and for now put all the trash in piles along the way, got it?"

"Got it." Deepak responds, "What are the animals going to do?"

"Pick up trash. I'm going to have a meeting with the birds, monkeys and other animals to explain everything to them. We'll spread the word all over the animal kingdom to pick up trash and add it to your piles. We hope that as the adults see what we are doing, they too will start cleaning up and before long, India will begin to see the importance of keeping their property clean."

"But then we'll just have big mounds of trash instead of trash all over. We're not really getting rid of the trash, we're just piling it up. That's not much of a solution." says Kashi.

"Point well taken, but God assured us he has a plan, and when God says he has a plan, it is best to not question it and just go along. If he wants us to gather up the trash, we'll do it. Are you with us?"

Deepak and Kashi look at each other in thoughtfulness before shrugging their shoulders.

"Okay, we'll do it. But I'm still not sure how?" says Kashi.

Hari smiles, "Go over behind that tree and you'll find an old tarp Madhuri and I picked up yesterday. It has a couple strings tied to it, so you both can use it to put your trash in. When it gets full, you can just dump it on the side of the trail and keep going for another load. While you're at school, the animals will be getting all this trash and putting it into one organized pile."

The two children run over to the tree and sure enough, there is a big blue tarp that seems a bit worn out, but perfect for their plan, so they pick it up and come back to the animals on the trail.

"This will work great." says the enthusiastic Deepak.

"Just find a good hiding place for it at school and near your home so every day you can use it to collect the trash."

"Okay." says Kashi, "Will you both be here every day?"

"We'll be here every morning to see how things are going and discuss anything that needs to be done." says Madhuri, "And of course, now that your angels are up to speed with the program," Hari looks at the kids wrists which are bare, "Did they not give you both the wristbands?" asks Hari in frustration.

Almost immediately, the wristbands appear on the children's arms as Hari closes his eyes and shakes his head, and the kids look at their new wristbands.

"Okay, let me explain the wristbands to you. You have a blue button," he says to Deepak, "And you have a pink button," he says to Kashi. "They have a G on it. If you push that button, it will connect you to your guardian angels immediately. I would recommend that you try not to use it. The green button with an A on it will connect you to Madhuri and I immediately. No matter where we are, we'll be able to talk to you. The other button with a DOG on it is for the Department of Greed which will connect you to an expert of greed who can help you out, but in your case, you are not likely to ever need it."

"This will be great." says Deepak, "But we do need to get to school, so we better move on."

"Yeah, you might want to start leaving your home a little earlier in the morning from now on, too. We don't want you to get in trouble with school."

"Okay Hari. Hope you and Madhuri have a great day." says the enthusiastic Kashi as they all move on, picking up trash as they go.

~~~~~~~~~~

"Get me Polly the Professor, please.

Will Polly the Professor please come to the control booth.

"And get Navin's guardian angel too please."

Will Navin's guardian angel come to the control booth as well please.

Polly enters first with Navin's angel close behind as God offers them both a seat.

"Thanks for coming. Polly, this is… Do you have a name, yet?" God asks Navin's angel.

"Yes sir, X34BDE" says the angel.

"Excuse me? Who gave you that name?" asks a flustered God.

"46QB8 sir. The angel in charge of name calling."

"Get me 4..6…QB8, please" God asks the angel at the door.

"Did you call for me sir?" asks 46QB8 as he walks into the booth.

"Yes. I would like to know why you called this angel X34BDE? That's not a name. It sounds like something out of NASA."

"Yes sir. That is my background sir." says 46QB8

"Excuse me?"

"Yes sir. I was the guardian angel for the scientist responsible for naming space objects like planets, comets, asteroids... objects that need a name. When the scientist passed over to this side, I was reassigned to the angel name calling department sir."

God is baffled as he takes a deep breath, "I want you to go back to the reassignment office and tell them you need to be assigned to some child with a gene pool full of scientists, okay?"

"Very well, sir."

As 46QB8 leaves, God tells the angel at the door, "Get me Mary."

"Yes sir."

"Did you call for me sir?" says Mary as she walks into the control booth.

"Yes, Mary. I understand you were a nurse at the maternity ward in England with a reputation of finding the perfect name for newborn children, is that correct?"

"Oh yes, sir. I loved finding the right name for the children."

"This is the guardian angel for Navin, a boy in India. What would you name him?" God asks as he presents X34BDE to Mary.

Mary looks the angel over in a very inquisitive way before looking to God.

"Jarred." she says with confidence.

God has a pained expression as he looks at X34BDE and then back to Mary.

"Why Jarred?" he asks.

"Oh I've always loved that name, sir. It's a very good name."

God pauses before he continues, "So if I were to assign you to the angel name calling department of earth operations, would you be calling all your angels Jarred?"

Mary laughs, "Of course not, sir. That would be most confusing. I would look at the child's family history, origin of birth and general background before I would name them. Since I didn't know anything about this angel, I just chose Jarred."

God smiles, "Excellent. I want you to report to the angel name calling department of earth operations right away please. I want you to start by recalling all the angels named by a 46QB8 and rename them with actual names. And remember, I want them to have names, not scientific formulas, alright?"

"Yes sir." says Mary as she turns and walks out to start her new adventure.

God looks back at the two angels and shakes his head, "Sorry for the interruption, but I had to nip that in the bud, you understand."

The two angels nod in agreement.

"So Polly, this is Jarred. He is the guardian angel of Navin, who is the son of a Rohit Malik, a good man who works for the Swachh Bharat Mission. They are an organization that is working to educate the India people on cleaning up their cities and villages throughout India. I need you to get

Bonnie's dad to contact Rohit to offer their garbage brick making process to the people of India. Jarred, I need you to work with Navin to convince his father that he would be a hero to get the brick making process going in India. Not only will it solve the issue of what to do with all the trash they are cleaning up, but the bricks can be used as a cheap resource for building material for the struggling people who live well below the poverty level. We need to move quickly on this, so let's get this going, alright?"

Polly and Jarred agree and walk out of the booth with a firm understanding of what needs to happen, as God sits back and smiles.

"X34BDE.... scientists. See what I mean about intellectual misgivings? This is exactly why I only want children and animals working this program." God stands to leave shaking his head and smiling, "Let me know if you need anything else." he says as he pats the back of the angel at the control panel, then pauses, "By the way, what is your name?" he asks the angel.

The angel shakes his head as he continues to monitor the activity below, "You don't want to know sir."

"Really?" God shakes his head, "What would you like to be named?"

The angel looks up at God and says, "I've always liked the name Norm." with a smile.

God pats him on the back again, "Okay. Norm it is from now on. Delete the memory of whatever it was they called you before. Keep up the good work, Norm." says God as he exits the booth.

"Thank you sir…. Thank you very much, sir."

~~~~~~~~~~

Kashi and Deepak have really made some progress in their trash pick up over the past several weeks. Every morning on their way to school, they leave piles of trash along the trail, and every afternoon on their way home, they find their piles of trash have been put together in one big pile by the animals. Some of the kids in their classroom have joined the effort as well as big blue tarps are easily found around the playground that are being used by the children to collect trash between their homes and the school every day, knowing that the animals will collect it all into one pile while they are in school.

The animals are having fun with it, too. They are all telling their children that so and so from their classroom is collecting way more trash, in order to crank up the competitive juices that always gets the best results with earthlings.

One morning, as Kashi and Deepak are making their way to school, they find Hari and Madhuri in their usual spot waiting for them.

"Hey, kiddos, how's the trash detail going today?" says Hari.

Kashi stops and seems a bit down, "You know Hari, we've been picking up trash on this same trail for a few of weeks now, and the pile just keeps getting bigger. We don't seem to be making any progress." She says.

Hari perks up, "Ah, but young lady, that's what Madhuri and I are here for. You and Deepak think you're not making any progress, but we can tell you that there are many children following your lead and collecting trash on their way to school. The animals are reporting that the mounds of trash being collected are growing like crazy, so don't be discouraged, kiddo."

"Well that sounds good, but all we're really doing is moving trash. What are we going to do with those mounds of trash that we are collecting?" asks the concerned Kashi.

Hari starts jumping up and down on Madhuri's back, "Do you want to tell her, or do you want me to big fella?" Hari asks Madhuri, but doesn't wait for an answer, "We found out that there is a family here from the United States who have sold a new machine that can convert all this trash into solid bricks that can be used to build homes for the many families that live in horrible shacks. They've already sold a lot of these machines to Brazil and they are using the bricks to build high rise farms and save the rain forests. Word is that the Swachh Bharat Mission plans to buy 100 of these machines and start making the bricks right away."

Deepak and Kashi look at each other then scream, "That is so cool!"

"They can put one of those machines right next to our pile of trash and within a day or two, turn that trash into piles of strong, environmentally friendly bricks that India can use to build homes for the poor or high rise farms for food." says Madhuri, "Of course they have all the fertilizer they need by collecting our poop, so the farms should produce some very good crops all over the country."

"That is so awesome!" says Kashi.

"So don't be discouraged, kiddos. Our plan is catching on and before you know it, everyone else will be looking at India as one of the cleanest, healthiest places to visit in the whole world." says Hari with a great deal of pride.

"Wow. So cool! We need to get to school. Thanks for making our day Hari and Madhuri!" says Deepak as the two children hurry off towards school.

~~~~~~~~~~

"Get me Leo, Furats guardian angel in here, will you Norm?" God asks as he makes his way to his seat.

The angel at the control panel looks up at God and smiles, "Yes, sir"

Will Leo, Furats guardian angel please report to the control booth please.

"Did you want to see me sir?" says the angel walking into the booth.

"Ah, yes Leo, come in and have a seat."

As Leo settles in, God asks, "Where did you get the name Leo?"

"Well, on my initial contact with Furat, I took on the physical presence of her favorite stuffed turtle named Leo, so I just let her call me Leo."

God smiles and looks over to Norm who is smiling as well with a 'thumbs up' response.

"Very good. Listen, I have another assignment for Furat.

I understand that the factory for this new form of transportation is doing very well, right?"

"Yes sir. They just really started production, but they are already getting a lot of orders from around the world."

"Excellent. So Amaan must be a happy man at this point?"

"Oh yes sir. He is very pleased."

"Good. I want you to get Furats dad, Saeed, to talk with the head of the factory and give him the plans I have created for a very cheap, environmentally friendly motor bike. If they see it as I do, they will have Saeed go back to Amaan to sell the idea of manufacturing these motor bikes for India and other places of poverty in exchange for the air polluting diesel bikes they are currently driving. They can be sold for practically nothing because they cost almost nothing to make. They can remove the air polluting bikes they have now and make money off of the recycled materials while Amaan will be called a hero in the environmental world while making his wealth all the greater."

"That sounds awesome, sir. How do I tell Furat to talk to her dad?"

"She needs to give him the idea that he should talk to the engineers at the factory about using the same technology on a simple motor bike to replace the diesel bikes and save the planet as well as make Amaan even richer. Then let Saeed take it from there. I'll make sure the engineer has very specific plans that make this happen, but of course, you didn't hear me say that, right?"

"Of course not."

God smiles, "India needs a lot of help if we are going to save the planet. I don't mind bending some of the rules I set up if it saves the planet."

"It's a great solution to the air quality issues sir, and I am hopeful that India will become a shining example to the rest of the world."

"Well it is a copy cat world they live in. Any time someone comes up with a new idea that not only makes them a hero with the tree huggers but also makes them a whole lot richer, you can bet everyone else is going to jump on that plan."

Leo gets up to leave, "If there's nothing else, I'll go visit Furat right away."

"Give her a hug for me… oh wait… you're a stuffed turtle, I guess that wouldn't work. Just let her know how much I appreciate her help."

"Will do, sir." says Leo as she heads out the door.

God sits back completely satisfied at how the CARPE DIEM Plan is going.

"How are things going in the rest of the world, Norm?" he asks.

"Very good. Like you say, it's a copy cat world they live in. Seems like everyone is trying to get in on the environmental bandwagon. Even China is going crazy trying to clean up their pollution."

God laughs, "China must be going crazy seeing India getting all the love." as he stands up to leave, "Well Norm, it looks like no rocks will be thrown today, right?"

"No rocks today, sir." responds Norm.

"And that's a good day, my friend. A very good day indeed." as God exits the control booth.

13

The Review

We are at the Earth Operations Headquarters in one of their large meeting rooms. God has called a meeting with the eight advisory angels to review the CARPE DIEM Plan and start planning the next step.

"I appreciate you all coming today, and am particularly pleased as I look around to see that each of you seem to have normal names." God says as he always has the angels wear name tags for any meetings because he has so many planets with so many life forms and keeping up with all the angels names can be an issue.

"So let's have a little fun before we start. How many of you had names given to you by an angel named," God pauses to look at his notes, "46QB8?"

They all raise their hands.

God sits back and smiles, "Oh my. Well I guess if your job is to name all the planets, asteroids, comets and other space objects, you learn to work fast, right? I'm curios to know what each of you were named before."

God looks at the angel to his left with a name tag that reads Alex.

"Alex?"

"AD74H9 sir."

God shakes his head, then looks to the angel next to Alex.

"Harry?"

"HP739F, sir"

"Tori?"

"TU4B83 sir"

"Maggie?"

"MC74Q8 sir"

"James?"

"JD735E sir"

"Betty?"

"BG74K7 sir"

"William?"

"WG76K3 sir"

"Zack?"

"Z.... sir"

"You forgot your name already?" God smiles.

"No sir. He named me Z sir."

"46QB8 named you Z?"

"Yes sir. We have some history sir." says the angel with a hint of hesitancy.

"Oh, do tell." says God as he leans over towards Zack to get the whole story.

"Well sir, when 46QB8 was the guardian angel for the scientist in charge of naming objects in space, I was the guardian angel of his assistant." says Zack.

"And?" says God waiting for more.

"Well sir, every time he named an object, I would tell him that it wasn't a proper name. At first, he would just show off his intellectual superiority by explaining how the name was based on a certain calculation and formula and was therefor a perfect name."

"And you disagreed?" God is loving this.

"Yes sir. I would usually just look at him and say again that this wasn't a proper name and then walk away. I wasn't going to argue with him."

"Sooooo....." says God in a prying way. "So when the assistant came over to this side and you went for reassignment, 46QB8 was in charge of names and called you Z?"

"Yes sir. He said it was a proper name, but in reality, it pretty much guaranteed that I would always be the last in line at the cafeteria."

God sits back in his chair howling with laughter.

"I've said it many times before that scientists are truly intellectual people, but only in a very narrow capacity. When it comes to being street smart, they pretty much have no clue. That's a good story right there." God is absolutely enjoying this story, "Tell you what I'm going to do for you Zack. I'm sending a memo to the cafeteria that says from now on the call list for meals shall not be alphabetical, but random within the angel community. And further more I will stipulate that my friend here, Zack, will never ever be permitted to be called last." he turns to Zack, "I would have said the same thing if I was the assistant. Well played, my friend."

"Thank you sir. Thank you very much." says Zack with great gratitude.

"Out of curiosity, did Mary explain your names when she gave them to you?"

"Harry?"

"She said since we had permanent roles here at EOH and would not be in the guardian angel program, she would just give us a name from the first letter of our formula names… and she let us have full approval."

"Nice." says God.

God leans back in his chair totally satisfied, "Well that pretty much does it for me. Anything else before we call it a day?"

"The CARPE DIEM Plan, sir?" says Betty, "We were called here to discuss the CARPE DIEM Plan."

God nearly falls out of his chair. "Of course. I apologize. I just get so wrapped up in these stories. That's why I love coming to Earth Operations Headquarters. You just can't beat the stories coming out of EOH, that's for sure."

God gathers himself and looks over his notes.

"Okay. I think it'd be best to go over each issue that caused us to create the CARPE DIEM Plan and make sure that we are doing all we can to get the issue headed in the right direction. I called this meeting because the plan seems to be going great on a general level. We can all agree that planet Earth is well on it's way back to a healthy existence. This meeting is not to pat ourselves on the back, but to take a very critical eye to make sure we are not missing anything. We need to establish the next phase of the plan, so it's important to first look at what has been done in a very thorough way."

God pauses and looks around the room to see that everyone is on the same page.

"First on my list is the poaching issue. I knew once I gave the animals the ability to understand and speak the language, they could easily stop the poaching on their own. I also know that we made a lot of headway into dismantling the black market rings of the supply chain. So I'm guessing that not only are the poachers not finding the animals, but the black market has pretty much been run out of business?"

"Maggie."

"Yes sir, there has been zero reports of poaching in the last two years."

The members clap in enthusiasm.

"And many of the poaching rings have been broken." says Maggie who is in charge of animal oversight at the EOH.

"How is the extension situation?" asks God.

"Not bad sir. We still have a few creatures that are endangered, but for the most part they are endangered merely because of the numbers – meaning more of them die each year under normal circumstances than are being born."

"They're not having enough babies?"

"No sir."

"Maybe we should we pipe in some nice Lou Rawls music for them?" asks God with a wink.

"Well the good news sir is that with the overall environment improvements, these animals death rates are slowing down now, so we are cautiously optimistic that the numbers will eventually begin to come back to a more normal level."

"Excellent. Does anyone else have anything else regarding the animals?" asks God.

"Alex?"

"Sir, it should be noted that the zoo that you used for our test run of the program has recently been credited with significantly reversing the situation with the White Rhinos. The problem with them was not just the low numbers, but there were not enough females being born to keep the reproduction cycles going. But with their new facility – called simply The Joey – they have been able to create a new generation of White Rhinos that have enough males and females to reproduce in a more normal cycle."

"Ah yes, The Joey. That was a great win for us to start with for sure. Anyone know how Nick is doing?"

Tori jumps in, "Yes sir. His company is leading the way in developing businesses that are environmentally friendly and financially profitable. And he and his wife have been great supporters of The Joey. The zoo is one of the great stories from our program sir."

"Oh that's great!" says God. "That's why I chose that to be our trial run. I could see in Nicks heart that he was a good man. I knew he had buried his memories of his dad always having to leave for business and how much it affected him. I knew he would wake up if we just nudged him a bit."

"Good news for the animals, which makes me very happy. I have mentioned to others that I may let the wild animals at least keep the ability to listen and understand language. I want at least one generation to grow up without hearing anything about poaching. Until I'm comfortable that the earthlings are going to be good stewards of the animals, I'll let the animals have the ability to protect themselves."

"Any other concerns or comments regarding the animals?" God asks.

"William?"

"Is the ability to listen and understand language going to be afforded to the domestic animals – or pets – and the animals at the zoos?"

"Good question. I'm leaning towards no on that. The domesticated pets don't need – or want, I suspect- to listen to the earthlings conversations. And the animals at the zoos are well taken care of by the keepers, so I wouldn't think it would be important for them. I would prefer to have the animals get back to a normal lifestyle as soon as possible, so my thinking is that only in the wild areas where poaching was a problem will we have the animals with the ability to hear and understand language. And just until we are all confident that poaching will not be coming back."

"Anything else?" God asks. The angels look around at one another and shake their heads no before God wraps it up, "I know that when I set up the CARPE DIEM Plan, that the poaching issue would be a fairly easy fix, so it's good to see the results reflecting that."

"How about the rain forests? Zack, I believe you are in charge of the trees and living plants department"

"Yes sir." says Zack as he looks at his notes, "The rain forests are bouncing back nicely as the Bonnie Bricks and mining issues have been developed. We've also found some developments from other areas. For instance, a young girl whose father is a plant scientist asked her father why they don't study the process of how trees filter the carbon and use the same principals in the factories that are spitting out the carbon into the atmosphere. Her father came up with a brilliantly simple process, that any factory could easily adapt to, that captures all the harmful carbons and recycles it with no impact on the environment. It's a brilliant process, sir, and it's catching on all over the planet."

"Excellent," says God, "You know there is not one mineral in the earth that a scientist couldn't duplicate in a lab. I put all the minerals in the earth for specific reasons and they need to remain in the earth. That's why I created trees, so carbon could be recycled back into the earth. The coltan, coal, silver, all the minerals I created were put into the earth for a reason. But the properties of all these minerals are fairly simple to duplicate in a lab. I did that on purpose too. I don't want the earthlings to strip out all the minerals. They need to stay in the earth's crust for so many reasons. It's about time that the earthlings are finally figuring this out."

God pauses before he continues, "So the deforestation of the rain forests is no longer a problem?"

Zack pauses, "Well I wouldn't say that it is no longer a problem, sir, but I would say that the issue is clearly headed in the right direction."

"Thanks Z…" God says with a smile.

"How about the water issue?" God says.

"Betty?"

"Well the ocean clean up is doing great. Once we got Bonnie's Blocks going, it seems like everyone wanted to help clean the oceans and rivers. The Reefs are bouncing back nicely, the aquatic animals are doing much better, and get this, sir," says Betty as she looks up and smiles at the group, "Bonnie's father created a processing machine that is small and simple to use that can be put on all ships – cargo ships, cruise ships, military ships – that fully recycles the waste into Bonnie Blocks that can be sold at any port of entry and help with the costs of running their companies. The amount of waste that is being dumped into the ocean is quickly being reduced."

The meeting breaks into applause and cat calls.

"Oh that's great, Betty. How about the rivers?" God asks.

"James?"

"India leads the way, sir, which is really good news because they were the worst. They have adopted several new methods to go with the Bonnie Blocks program in order to clean up their rivers and lakes. It has worked so well that many other countries are adopting the same methods, so I think it is safe to say that the entire planet's water system is well on its way to a healthier level."

"Excellent!" says God with great enthusiasm.

"How about the air quality?"

"Harry?"

"Sir the new transportation systems that Amaan's motor company created has really taken off. There are new companies all over the world creating these new systems to replace the polluting cars and trucks. It looks like they are saying that within ten years time, the automobile will be a thing of the past. When you combine this with the rejuvenation of the rain forests, and the overall health of the planet, not only has the air quality greatly improved, but the weather cycles have stabilized to a much more normal pattern. We are very encouraged by the progress of the air quality."

"This is all very good news." says God, "Does anyone have any issues that need to be looked at?"

"Tori?"

"Yes sir. The political issue could still present us some problems. There are a lot of companies that are jumping onto the environmental bandwagon, but some of the governments are resisting the changes. These countries that are resisting are for the most part the countries that need to change the most."

"Yes, that's possibly the greatest issue we have to face." says God, "This is why I said the main ingredient to the CARPE DIEM Plan is that we needed to change hearts, not just behaviors. The gap between the haves and the have nots will always be a problem. Let's not kid ourselves. We didn't do anything to change Amaan's heart, we just gave him the opportunity to get wealthier. Without changing the hearts, we are simply creating more divisiveness between those who have the wealth and power and those who do not. The CARPE DIEM Plan will never sustain a positive outcome unless we change hearts. We may not change every heart, but we will never be able to claim victory until we know that we have changed enough hearts to secure the future health of the planet."

"Excuse me, sir, but we have a situation that needs your immediate attention." says an angel who comes into the room in a rush.

"What is the issue?" says God as he turns his attention to the angel.

"Sir, India and China are holding meetings with the military personnel and it appears that war is imminent."

"Really? What is the issue?"

"It seems that India has been accusing China of stealing their formulas for cleaning the rivers and lakes without paying them and China is refusing to pay for anything."

"So they will bomb the hell out of each other and that will solve the issue, right?" God says shaking his head.

"There is no love lost between these two countries sir." says the angel.

God looks back at the others around the table.

"Okay. Maggie, you and Alex go get every animal you possibly can to gather around the buildings in India and

China where these meetings are being held. I don't want them to do anything but surround the buildings and stare at it in a calm, relaxed manner, understood?"

As the two get up, Maggie says to Alex, "You take China and I'll get India." as they leave the room in a rush.

"William, you and Tori get the guardian angels of all the children of India and China and have them get the children to the buildings where these meetings are taking place. I want them to be quiet and stand still with the animals. We don't have a lot of time, so don't worry about it. Get as many children as possible to those buildings to stand with the animals."

As they both get up to leave, Tori says, "I got China, you get India." as they head out the door.

"The rest of you get over to the control booth at the CARPE DIEM command center and get everyone on full alert. If you come up with any ideas while you're monitoring the situation, don't waste time trying to clear it with me. If the four of you like it, do it."

"What about you, sir?" asks the angel.

God gets up and heads to the door.

"I'm going to serve the water." he says as he exits.

14

Bombs Away

God makes his way out of the kitchen with a pitcher of water. He is dressed in a fancy black tuxedo with a white linen draped over his forearm. He makes his way to the main table of a meeting room in the China government building where many military dignitaries have gathered with the President and his advisors.

""Sorry I'm running a little behind, fellas, but I have the water ready to go now." he says in a very disruptive and annoying manner.

As they all turn to watch him, God continues to pour the water with an on-going array of "How ya doin'?", "Good to see you." and "Glad you could make it."

The high ranking officials look at God, then at their water, which appears to be some sort of muddy gunk.

"Who is this man?" says the President.

"Oh, excuse me, Mr. President. I am God. I came as soon as

I heard about the meeting." God says as he continues to pour the sludgy water.

"Call security!" says the President.

"Oh, Mr. President, I would highly recommend you not be doing that sir." as God stops pouring and looks at the President, "Being God, I have the ability to be seen and heard by whoever I want to see or hear me, and I assure you the security detail will not be seeing or hearing me."

As he is speaking, a handful of heavily armed security personnel run through the door and towards the main table, looking every direction for any dangerous activity. One of the security guards runs right through God without flinching.

"Did you call, sir?" says one of the security guards.

The President looks perplexed at the security guard who ran right through God, "Did you not see…"

"I wouldn't go there, Mr. President." God cuts the President off, "He didn't see me. He didn't feel me. And he can't hear me. I strongly recommend that you release the security people so we can get on with our meeting." God says with a big smile as he stares at the President, who is baffled.

After an uncomfortable pause, the President turns to the security commander and says, "No. It was a false alarm. Please take the security unit away."

"Yes sir." says the security commander as he signals the unit to stand down and leave the room.

"I hear the banana muffins in the cafeteria are excellent." yells God to the unit as they are leaving.

"Ah, most unfortunate. They still can't hear me." says God as he turns and heads up to the President.

"Please, sit down. I know that you all have a lot to talk about, but since I am the one who created this planet – which technically means I own it – I took it upon myself to show up and give you a few thoughts from my perspective before you discuss your options."

God gets to the President who remains standing and has a look of indignant interruption.

"We do not believe in God." he says with authority.

"I know, please sit down Mr. President." says God as he pulls out the chair for the President. "And that's the rub, isn't it?" God says, "On the one hand I have China that doesn't believe in any God, wanting to go to war with India that has way too many Gods. And here I am in the middle thinking that this is going to be a tough crowd, right?"

As if on cue, there is no response.

"Exactly." says God as he leans over the Presidents shoulder an pushes a button and a big screen comes out of the ceiling. When it stops, there is a couple of blinks before the screen shows a live video feed of what appears to be a meeting in India, as the Prime Minister is sitting at the head of the table with military personnel sitting around a table. They are all staring at the camera unaware of what is going on.

"I know what you all are thinking. How did he get that video feed, right? Well I have to admit that you both did me a huge favor because both these rooms have already been bugged by each of you so it really wasn't that difficult for me

to simply add a video feed to what you already had in place."
God says as both the China and India meetings look around
at each other in horror.

"Now in order to get our friends in India up to speed, I
was telling the good people here in China that I am God.
Of course, the Chinese don't believe in God and you good
people of India have so many Gods, I really don't have a
chance.

"So I thought I'd start this meeting by doing a little trick
that will hopefully get us past the issue of God, and get
us talking about the real issue at hand. Now, when I was
pouring the water for you fellas here in China, the glasses in
India were filling up with the same water."

God pauses as everyone in the meetings are looking at their
glasses of sludge.

"As you can see, the water doesn't look very refreshing I
would say. But did you know, that with a simple snap of my
fingers, (God snaps his fingers) these awful looking glasses of
water suddenly becomes refreshing, cool, quenching glasses
of water that we certainly could use at a meeting like this."
God pours himself a glass of water and drinks it down.

"Aw yes, now that is a refreshing glass of water, there. You
are all welcome to enjoy the water, please."

Only a few actually take a sip, raising their eyebrows in
surprise before they have another sip.

"Now I don't pretend to think that a glass of water is going
to convince you all that I am the one true God. It's what I
think marketing people call an ice breaker or something silly

like that. I have no plans to do any more tricks for you people, because I know you are both anxious to get this war thing going.

"So let me get this straight. India, you are pissed off at China because they stole – according to you – your formula for cleaning your polluted air, is that correct?"

The members of the India meeting look around at each other before the PM slowly nods in agreement, with great hesitation.

"I'll take that as a yes. Thank you."

"And China, I believe there is not one country on this planet that is not aware of the thievery that your country practices. Now, some of it is mostly a matter of taking a good idea and creating your own version, which is perfectly fine, but there are plenty of instances that we can point to as sheer unadulterated thievery, am I correct China?"

All the people in the India meeting nod their heads yes with gusto as the people in China puff up their chests in a defensive manner.

"Okay, let me use a parable her – I love using parables you know.

"Little Johnny and little Suzie are playing in a sandbox. Johnny comes running up to his mother and cries, 'Mommy, Suzie took my shovel and won't give it back' so Johnny's Mother calls to Suzie 'Did you take Johnny's shovel, Suzie?' and Suzie says, 'He wasn't using it and I didn't know it was his.' she says. Johnny's mother looks to Johnny and asks, 'Is that shovel yours Johnny?' to which he answers, 'No, but I wasn't done using it.'"

"Now you are all very good when you are raising your children to teach them to share and to be honest, right? So why don't we just go back to our childhood and look at this situation again."

God looks to the screen at the people in India, "Tell me, India, do you own the formula that cleans your air?"

The Prime Minister says, "We paid a lot of money for that formula!"

"Ah, yes you did. But the formula belongs to whom?"

"Well, we bought it…"

God interrupts the Prime Minister,

"Let me help you out, sir. You paid a good price for the Bonnie Blocks company to make you the machines needed to process all your trash, and you paid Amaan Motor Bike Company, a handsome price for all the transportation units to replace the old, filthy motor bikes, is that correct?"

"Well, yes, but China stole the formulas from us."

As both rooms start to escalate God cuts them both off, "Hold on here. If I can have security people running through me without flinching, I can certainly make it so none of you have a voice. But I am not only God, I am a reasonable God. So please, everyone sit down and take a sip of this refreshing water."

God waits as a spattering of the officials take a sip from their glass.

"Okay, so let's review. India, you are willing to push the

button that will throw a bunch of nuclear warheads towards China because they stole something that actually doesn't belong to you in the first place. And China, you are willing to push your buttons that will throw a bunch of nuclear warheads towards India because they accused you of stealing, which in fact, is true.

"Now the objects that you are willing to obliterate each other over are formulas and processes that are designed to clean up your environment and provide your people with a much healthier lifestyle, which both countries desperately need."

God pauses to let this sink in.

"I certainly hope that there are a few people in this room – and there in India – who can see the irony of this scenario you both have created.

"India, you have taken some major steps forward in your effort to clean up your country. I would hope that all of you in that room today would take great pride in the progress you have made in bringing back India to the wonderful clean land of enchantment that it was created to be.

"And China, I know you are committed to cleaning up your country as well and these formulas you have, should I say, BORROWED, will be a great help to your country. I will personally see to it that the Bonnie Bricks company and Amaan Motor Bike Company reach out to you and provide you with these wonderful inventions at a fair price that I am confident you will see as a wise investment for your people."

God looks around at both rooms and sees a bunch of military men frozen in their seats afraid to make any move.

"Let me further assure you both that because I am God, and neither of you believe in me, I will guarantee you both that if either one of you pushes a button to release those missiles towards the other, I will personally redirect every missile to head harmlessly into outer space and never, ever do harm to anything. You might want to reconsider.

"Well I know you all are anxious to get to your meeting, but let me just say that I could have turned that water into wine," he pauses and smiles, "I make an excellent champagne, but I only use it for meetings that result in something positive to celebrate. Meetings that talk about wars and destroying your neighbors just get water."

God looks around the rooms again.

"But before I leave, let me ask you to do one more thing for me. I want each and every one of you to get out of your seats and come over to these windows."

God looks around as nobody moves a muscle.

"Okay, where I come from there are no clocks because I live in eternity. But you all don't, so let me make the instructions clearer. I want each and every one of you to get out of your seats NOW and come stand at these windows ... India, you need to get up and stand at your windows as well."

Slowly, they get up and make their way to the windows that look out over their cities. When they get to their windows, their eyes grow twice as wide and their jaws drop open in disbelief as they see a sea of children and animals quietly standing and staring up at them. There is an uncomfortable quiet in both cities. No traffic, no horns, no hustle and bustle. Just faces of children and animals standing quietly and looking up at the leaders.

"I know that your two countries don't believe in me. I am the one who gave you all free wills. That's okay. I'm not asking you to do anything for me. I have lots of planets with lots of activities going on. I'll be fine. But I want you to look at those faces down there and understand that this is THEIR planet. Whatever you decide today will have an affect on those faces and their future. You damn well better make the right decision today, fellas. Those are my children. Those are my animals. This is my planet.

"Do the right thing today." says God as he walks out of the room, leaving both India and China looking out their windows at the faces of children and animals looking to them for hope.

~~~~~~~~~~

BREAKING NEWS

In a surprise move today, India and China have agreed to stand down on their military build up against each other and instead work together as partners to improve the environment for future generations. We have reports from both capitols. First this report from William Jakes in New Delhi.

Thanks Judy.

I am outside the government building where the meeting of the Prime Minister and military advisors completed about an hour ago. Most everyone was expecting to hear the Prime Minister give details of how India was going to proceed with military action against China, but instead, the Prime Minister announced a new joint effort to work with China to improve the environment throughout the Asian continent.

Nobody saw this coming, Judy, as almost everyone expected the meeting in New Delhi as well as Beijing to result in a formal declaration of war between the two countries.

This is a developing story, so for now, let me toss it over to Crystal in Beijing.

Thanks, William.

I am outside the military complex where we recently heard from the President of China about the agreement that has been reached between India and China. There is a very positive energy around the square here in Beijing as most people had no idea that this would be the results from these meetings. Nobody saw this coming, Judy.

On a side note, a lot of people are talking about all the children and animals that showed up here during the meeting. As far as you could see there were animals and children standing together looking up at the windows where the meeting took place. We understand that the same thing happened in New Delhi. No one knows who organized the gathering of children and animals, but it certainly was an impressive and powerful sight, to say the least.

There are a lot more questions than answers at this point, Judy, but for now, we can only show this picture of both meetings holding up what appears to be glasses of Champagne and saluting each other on their live video feeds.

Quite an amazing development today.

Judy, back to you.

Thanks Crystal, an amazing development indeed.

Now for more reaction throughout the world…..

15

Victory Is Ours

The Cloud Nine Assembly Hall is rocking tonight. All the guardian angels at Earth Operations Headquarters are gathered to hear Gods plan for planet earth moving forward. Everyone knows that the CARPE DIEM Plan was a huge success, so the atmosphere is electric.

The band is keeping the angels in party mode and God seems to be in no hurry to break the atmosphere. God loves his angels. He knows he asked them to go well beyond their comfort zone with the CARPE DIEM Plan. Angels were not designed to be emotional. To work in the guardian angel program at Earth Operations, you have to have a good understanding of emotions, but when you are assigned a new earthling, God felt it would be vital for the angels to be more practical and have a calming spirit when working the day to day operations with the emotional earthlings.

The CARPE DIEM Plan made many of the guardian angels do things that they were not accustom to doing. All the names. All the physical images they needed to take on. All the quick decisions they needed to make. God understood that these angels were not exactly designed for something like the CARPE DIEM Plan. He understood that a guardian angel was only responsible for one earthling at a time and they were designed to remain focused on the one earthling until they crossed over.

God knows that these angels are happy to see the CARPE DIEM Plan come to a close, so he is in no hurry to break up the party atmosphere.

"Ladies and gentlemen. Please give it up for your own creator.... the author of love .... the God who put Earth on the map ... your very own master of love-ins ... God Almighty!"

As the band crashes into 'You Ain't Seen Nothin' Yet' the angels jump from their seats and explode with cheering and celebration as God walks out to the podium. God, once again, is in no hurry to cut off this celebration, so he stands back and lets the angels party.

But a good band knows when it is time to put a wrap on the party, so God makes his way to the podium as the music concludes and the angels take their seats.

"Thank you all for coming. This is one celebration you all deserve, and I am not one to cut corners when it comes to partying."

A nice round of applause.

"But before we party, we do need to look at what we have done and take a moment to appreciate the power of love.

When I started the CARPE DIEM Plan, I know many of you thought that I had a choice between throwing a rock at the planet, or come up with a plan to solve the problems. I can tell you today that I did not have a choice. My whole existence is built on Love. My love is unconditional. At no point was there any thought of throwing a rock at planet earth. It was never a choice between the two options, it was only a matter of understanding the problem and looking at what we need to do fix the problem.

"I will never throw rocks at my creations!"

The angels explode with approval.

"As I look back on the many events that were a part of the CARPE DIEM Plan, the first takeaway I have is how much you guardian angels had to work outside your comfort zone. I realized that when I created the guardian angel program here at Earth Operations, I designed the guardian angels to have a focus on one earthling at a time, one life at a time. We can – and should – look back and have a few laughs at the many obstacles you angels had to adjust to, knowing that you were never created to make those adjustments. I had angels flying from Brazil to San Diego. I had angels having to create names for animals, coming up with names like Snake, Bird, Spider and Howler. I had angels taking a lot of heat because in a pinch, they had to take over a cute little man on a bottle of soap in order to get a message to their earthling. I want each and every one of you angels to hear me when I say that I truly understood that you were asked to do many things you were not created to do, but even though there were some trying times, I never lost faith in my angels. I never doubted for a minute that my angels were up to the task. I never ... EVER ... felt that my angels would not come through.

"The CARPE DIEM Plan worked because of YOU.

"Thank You!"

The band breaks into celebration as the angels go wild, high fiving each other as God claps and points to the angels and claps more. But the band knows when to stop, and stop they do.

God steps up to the podium again to continue but takes a moment to take in the scene.

"Nothing serves love more than watching so many angels working together, often under difficult circumstances, for a single purpose. As you all know, I have plenty of planets. I could easily have reassigned each of you to another system. But we all had one love for planet Earth. And it is that love that brought us here today to celebrate. I could never express my deepest appreciation I have for the love you angels continue to show to your earthlings. You are the reason I knew the CARPE DIEM Plan would work."

"Thank You!"

The band breaks into another rock'n version of 'All We Need Is Love" as God steps back to let the angels have their moment.

As he watches the angels celebrate, he thinks about the many events that unfolded during the CARPE DIEM Plan. He thinks about the many issues that seemed so hopeless before and how these angels did so much to create the solutions that should have planet earth in a healthy state for generations to come. He thinks about his children and animals working together to show the adults how to be good stewards of their planet.

It's been a wild ride saving the planet. It's still a free will planet, so the future is never guaranteed. But God looks at the planet differently now. There will be adjustments moving forward. There are still obstacles that need to be addressed. But as God looks out at all his guardian angels celebrating and thinks about the events that have unfolded, he knows one thing is certain....

YOU NEVER THROW ROCKS AT SOMETHING YOU LOVE

God had to make a choice.

God always chooses LOVE.

~~~~~~~~~~

The United Nations Environmental Program came out with a report today that shows for the fifth year in a row, the environmental readings on a global scale have improved again this year. As Lisa Baylor tells us in this report, every category of environmental concern has shown improvement again this year. Lisa

Thanks Judy.

The report has been met with great enthusiasm by many world leaders who have come out in unanimous support for the many programs that have turned the environmental issues around. I spoke with Bonnie Johnson, the US Ambassador to the United Nations who has been one of the leaders of the environmental movement.

This is the fifth year in a row that we have had a positive report on the environment, Ms Johnson. How significant is this report on a global scale?

"It's very significant because it shows improvement on every issue of the environment. Our oceans continue to respond to the cleanup efforts. Coral reefs are bouncing back to life, the many species of aquatic life continue to grow in a healthy environment. Our agricultural programs are showing great progress. The rain forests are again stabilizing with little deforestation concerns. The animal kingdom has shown a great turnaround in the endangered species as poaching and wild life management has made great progress. And the air pollution has provided again this year very clean atmospheric readings, and the extreme weather patterns we were experiencing has stabilized a great deal. We should all be encouraged."

What do you contribute this turnaround to?

"Hearts. We always had the ability to solve the problems, but we needed to change hearts to commit to a process that would make it happen. The more hearts you win over, the more commitment you have to solving the problems. We have won a lot of hearts and this report shows us what we can do when we put our hearts into an issue."

Well Judy, it's been another great report for our planet and tomorrow, I'll have a report on the many side affects in our day to day living that has come from a clean environment.

Back to you Judy.

Thanks, Lisa for that encouraging report. In other news....

The End

It's never too late to turn this story to non-fiction!